~ Even the most overlooked can effect change

The ability to communicate with dragons is essential for competitive dragon racing. So, when Jackson McLoughlin is born into a family of Dragon Speakers and lacks this gift, he is labeled Creature Deaf.

Now a teenager, Jackson is left to increasingly question his worth as his family struggles to stay competitive against a well-funded racing conglomerate.

When an overwhelming urge leads Jackson to save Tivet, an abused dragonet, something happens that neither of them expected. But as the unlikely duo explore their growing bond, corrupt forces are gaining a foothold within their small racing community.

Can Jackson and Tivet restore a once-champion dragon's confidence in time to save the McLoughlin family's farm?

LABYRINTH OF RUIN

SHELLEY LEE RILEY

Runner-up Publishing
United States, United Kingdom, Australia

Runner-up Publishing

Illustrator: Ionescu Mihai Dan (Fiverr: funkwave)

Paperback ISBN: 978-0-9863939-6-9

eBook ISBN: 978-0-9863939-7-6

LABYRINTH OF RUIN

SHELLEY LEE RILEY

JACKSON TURNED THE VOLUME DOWN for the third time only to have his brother flick it back up.

"What's got into you?"

"I thought I heard something." Jackson turned the radio off. Using a pair of vice grips, he rolled down the truck's rickety window. "Can't you hear it?"

"Nope." Robby braked on a sharp turn made slick after a recent rain shower. "Look at that." His voice was breathy with wonder. "We've found the end of the rainbow."

A kaleidoscope of colors sparkled under the Irish sun, turning the windshield into a giant prism, nearly blinding in its intensity. Jackson's eyes widened in wonder.

"I guess it's our lucky day." Robby laughed. "But where's the pot of gold?"

Jackson didn't answer. Suddenly doubled over, he clutched his chest. Pain, grinding in its intensity, stole his breath.

⁂

ROBBY EASED THE TRUCK OFF the road and leaned over to grip

his younger brother's shoulder. "What's wrong, Jack?" The bones beneath Robby's fingers felt far too fragile. Jackson may have been thirteen, but he resembled a weedy ten-year-old.

"Talk to me," Robby said, trying to get a better look at the smaller boy's face. The warm spattering of freckles that dotted his cheeks stood in stark relief as Jackson's normal color continued to wash away. Robby's gut twisted with concern.

Drawing in a shuddery breath, Jackson sat up. "It's gone."

"Gone?" Robby straightened. "What do you mean, *it's gone?* You looked like you were going to puke your guts out."

"Yeah, well, it wasn't sick I was feeling."

"Just gas, then, huh?" Robby tweaked Jackson's nose, relieved but not wholly mollified.

"Shut up." Jackson batted his brother's hand away.

Settling back behind the wheel, Robby eyeballed a colorful encampment up ahead. "Well, look there, the Travellers are back in town. That'll put a burr up the village council's backsides."

⁂

JACKSON LOOKED WHERE ROBBY POINTED. Several brightly-colored caravans, both new and old, filled the wide spot along the verge. From experience, Jackson knew that a small brook ran through the spinney that bordered the clearing, which was why the Travellers chose the site whenever they were in the area.

When he and his mum had come into town the week prior, the space had been empty. And yet, even over such a short period, it had become cluttered. Old propane tanks, wooden crates, discarded clothing, and a rusted-out washing machine were among the many things piled off to one side.

"Why do they transport that stuff only to throw it away? It makes no sense," Robby mused.

A flicker of motion caught Jackson's attention. He leaned forward in his seat as a gaggle of children burst from the woods, screaming in delight as they chased each other with wooden swords. Sporting flowered aprons tied around their necks, their make-believe capes billowed as they scampered about waving their weapons.

Jackson felt a pang of longing. They looked like they were having fun. Dragon farms tended to be rural. And since his three brothers had yet to marry, there weren't any other kids for him to play with.

"Are you all right then, boyo?" Robby playfully tugged at one of Jackson's coppery curls. "Do we need to head home? Or can you hang on long enough to pick up the dragon feed at the abattoir? You know they don't like to hold the big orders overnight."

"No, I'm fine. I don't know what came over me."

"Can you describe what it felt like?" Glancing over his shoulder, Robby pulled the truck back onto the blacktop. They didn't have far to go.

"I thought I heard something, but it wasn't like words. More like a feeling."

"What kind of feeling?"

"Desperation." Jackson rubbed his breastbone. "I couldn't breathe."

"Dang, that's harsh. You sure you're okay?"

"Yeah, I am."

Ten minutes later, Robby signaled before pulling into the customer pick-up line at C & J Meat Packing, where three other trucks already waited.

"It looks like it'll be a while." Robby shut off the motor.

Most dragon trainers had their feed delivered, but a few, like McLoughlin Racing Stables, still preferred to pick up their orders.

"Guarantees it's fresh and right off the line." The brothers laughed as they simultaneously recited their da's favorite dictum. It wasn't like they went inside to retrieve the meat. It rolled out to the loading dock on a conveyor belt. Who knew how long it sat there before it finally ended up in the bed of their truck?

"Since we're going to be here for a while, would you be okay with going to the mercantile by yourself?"

"Yeah." Jackson opened the door.

"Wait. Have you got enough *dosh*?" Robby smiled, reaching for his wallet. "New boots don't come cheap."

"Mum gave me what she said I would need. '*And not a pingin' more.*'" Jackson shook his finger at his brother, mimicking their mother.

Robby laughed at his brother's impersonation. "Still, you sure you don't want another ten quid, kiddo?"

"Nah." They both knew they couldn't afford the fifty pounds Jackson had tucked in the pocket of his jeans. But he'd been wrapping duct tape over the ever-widening holes in the soles of his boots for some time. Dragon urine was pretty caustic stuff.

"I'm going to stop by the Oxfam store first. You never know. I might find something that fits for a third of the price. Then I won't have to buy new ones. If I get really lucky, they might have a set of Wellies without big cracks in the rubber."

"If you didn't wade around in the slurry pit, your boots would last longer."

"Oh yeah? And who would be emptying the pits if I didn't do it, Robby? You?" Jackson snorted as he slipped out of the cab and, with a big grin, flashed his older brother a rude gesture.

CHAPTER TWO

JACKSON SIGHED AS HIS BROTHER continued to ogle his next-to-new boots.

"For the last time, I didn't steal them. Cara, the shop manager, found them in a donation box from the Sinclair's. She figured they'd fit and put them aside for me."

"Cara? You know the shop manager by her first name? She cute?" Robby teased.

"I'm not you," Jackson shot back. "Besides, she's got grandkids. She likes me."

"The Sinclair's? Dang, Jack, those boots probably cost more than two hundred quid. They look brand new. Must've come right off their daughter's feet."

Jackson shouldered past his brother and climbed into the rusty heap they used to haul the dragon feed. Crossing his arms, he stared sullenly at Cassie's boots. Knowing she'd been wearing them when she'd been thrown from her horse wasn't something he wanted to think about.

Robby got into the driver's seat but waited before starting the engine. "I'm sorry, I shouldn't have said that. It wasn't funny."

"No, it wasn't." Jackson broke his silence. "Cassie was a nice girl. I liked her a lot." His frown deepened. "She was the only one of those rich kids that didn't pinch her nose when I came into class. I've almost gotten used to being called Dragon Butt."

"Sometimes I forget how obnoxious those little snots can be at that pretentious academy." Robby turned the key in the ignition, and the diesel engine roared to life.

"It's not like there was anywhere else to go after the village school closed."

"And yet, you and the dentist's son, Kevin, get your nose rubbed in it daily, even though the council forced the academy to admit you guys." Robby muscled the heavily loaded truck back onto the road.

"Yeah, whatever." Jackson squirmed. He stared at the pebble-dash exteriors of the cottages clustered near the edge of town. "I don't care what they think."

"Is there anything else in that bag besides your worn-out boots? It looks kind of full." Robby changed the subject.

"A pair of Wellies, and if I wear an extra pair of socks, they shouldn't get sucked off in the muck."

"It sure turned out to be your lucky day. You need to keep on flirting with those older ladies."

"Shut your gob, Robby. You're the one the lavender-haired crowd swoons over at the spring festival."

"And that shows women don't lose their good taste with age."

Jackson rolled his eyes so hard it was a wonder he wasn't staring at the back of his skull.

"What can I say? It's a gift." Robby playfully poked his brother in the ribs.

Jackson doubled over.

"Hey, I barely touched you."

"Pull over. Gonna be sick." Jackson opened the door and jumped out before the truck entirely stopped. Bent over, he retched until it felt like his insides were coming out.

"What's up with you?" Robby stood over Jackson, gently patting his back. "Touch of the stomach flu?"

Jackson used the back of his hand to wipe his mouth. It was the same pain and overwhelming anguish he'd felt on the way into town. Straightening up, he looked across the road toward the Travellers' colorful encampment.

"Hey, where you going?" Robby grabbed Jackson's shoulder as he started to cross the road. "I can't leave the meat unattended."

Jackson shrugged off his brother's hand. "I'll be right back."

CHAPTER THREE

NO ONE PAID JACKSON ANY MIND as he wound his way to the back of the encampment. He didn't know how he knew where he needed to go. Jackson didn't question it. He just knew it was where he *had* to go.

He stopped before an older, barrel-shaped caravan, the type commonly seen hitched to a pair of the distinctive black and white Irish Cobs that the Travellers preferred. Jackson didn't see the horses around, but he heard a commotion coming from the far side of the caravan.

What he found when he rounded the end of the wagon stopped him in his tracks. The children he'd seen earlier playing with wooden swords had cornered a strange-looking creature. Shrieking with laughter, they took turns poking the cowering animal with their sharpened sticks.

"Hey. What's going on?" Jackson called out. The kids stopped and turned on him.

"None of your business, Towny." The apparent leader of the pack stepped up to confront Jackson, eyeing him up and down. "What makes you think you can sashay in here . . ." The sneer on the boy's face was far from friendly. "Sportin' them fancy, girly boots?" The bully pushed further into Jackson's personal space.

Even though he should've considered protecting himself, Jackson couldn't take his eyes off the dark creature huddled against the spokes of one of the wagon's wheels.

"What've you got there?" Jackson ignored the boy's insults and pointed toward the creature.

"Like I said, it ain't none of your business." Several inches taller than Jackson, the kid shoved him. "We don't like no Townies in our camp. You best get on home to your mommy, *Girly Boy*."

"Not until you tell me what you lot are tormenting." Jackson clenched his fists.

The boy raised his sword.

"Stop," a gruff voice announced the arrival of an adult. "What do you think you're doing, Toby? We don't start no trouble with Townies. You know better."

"He," Toby waved his sword in Jackson's face, "just waltzed in like he owned the place and started interfering in our business."

"Is that so?" Big and swarthy, the man put his hand on Jackson's shoulder. "What do you want, boy?"

"Him." Jackson pointed toward the creature.

"Him?" The man wasn't just big; he was massive and didn't look to be the forgiving type. But Jackson was beyond caring.

"Yes, I want him. How much?"

"How much you got?"

Jackson pulled a crumpled five-pound note from his pocket.

"That ain't gonna buy you no dragon."

CHAPTER FOUR

WHEN ROBBY'S BROTHER RETURNED from the Travellers' camp, he was barefoot, and leading the most pitiful excuse for a baby dragonet Robby had ever seen.

"What in all that is holy is that supposed to be?" Robby straightened from where he'd been leaning against the truck's front fender. "And where are your new boots?"

"He's worth it," Jackson stated flatly.

"He?" Robby's black eyebrows nearly touched his hairline. "Don't you mean it? What is it, anyway?"

"Very funny. As you can plainly see, it's a dragonet."

"That's no dragonet, Jackson. It's a dried-up husk unfit for feeding a pack of wild dogs. Take it back and get your boots." Robby reached for the frayed lead rope wrapped around the dragonet's scrawny neck. "Never mind, I'll do it. I won't stand for traveling trash cheating my brother."

"No!" Jackson fell to his knees, wrapped his arms around the pitiful creature, and burst into tears. "Please, Robby, don't take him away from me. I need him."

Robby stilled. He'd never seen his brother cry. And

Jackson wasn't crying. He sobbed into the neck of the pathetic excuse for a dragonet. But it was when the wizened little animal unfurled his torn wings and wrapped them around his brother that Robby's decision became undeniable.

"I know I'm going to live to regret this," Robby huffed. "Fine, help me put him in the backseat. He looks far too weak to get up there on his own."

CHAPTER FIVE

JACKSON'S ANXIETY RATCHETED HIGHER as he counted down the stacked stone mile markers on their way back to the farm. The beauty of the emerald green fields didn't distract him. With unclipped tails flapping as they gamboled in the sparkling sunlight, the spring lambs didn't register either—just the countdown to the confrontation waiting at the end of the road.

There was no question what his father's reaction would be to the surprise arrival of a baby dragonet. As the miles ticked by, Jackson kept asking himself what his response would be when the inevitable happened, and his da said Tivet couldn't stay.

It wasn't like Jackson didn't understand that times were tough and that it wasn't just the case for his family's farm.

The stories told around the dinner table and repeated at the village hall were about how it had always been. How Northern Ireland dragon trainers, like Jackson's family, were content to stay within their region and rarely challenged the long-standing dominance held by more prominent trainers on the international scene. There was a good reason for dragon racing being labeled the Sport of Kings.

That didn't mean, on occasion, a racing dragon, capable of competing with the high flyers, wasn't raised locally. But once a dragon displayed that kind of talent, the bloodstock agents came calling, money in hand.

Dragon Speakers and their families had thrived within this symbiotic relationship for generations. Small purses and training fees kept them going, but the occasional influx of dosh from selling a next-level dragon guaranteed stability.

At least, that's how it had been until sports betting began expanding, allowing punters to bet on their favorite dragons from every corner of the world. With a percentage of the betting handle injected into the purses, vast amounts of money were on the line. And where the money was, the big racing conglomerates followed. With their extensive stables and unlimited means, they soon became the dominant players—in some cases, even nudging out the royals.

Despite that, local racing had changed little. If anything, with the continued expansion of racing in other countries, the demand for racing prospects had only increased. And life had looked good for the locals until Duffy Nolan established an outpost in their region.

Nolan Racing Stable epitomized the corporate side of racing. His presence pressured local, generational racing families out of business, and Nolan quickly gobbled up these failed farms. From the angry voices raised at the meetings in the village hall, Jackson knew more families were teetering on the edge and were considering selling out to Nolan as their only option before they lost everything.

Jolted from these grim thoughts, Jackson braced himself as the truck lurched to a stop in the farm's turnabout. They climbed out and with trepidation, Jackson watched Robby quietly lift the sad little creature from the back seat and set him on the packed gravel surface where Da waited.

Cullum didn't say a word, just crossed his beefy arms as

his hawk-eyed stare took in the trio before him.

"His name is Tivet." Jackson stumbled, nearly falling, as ragged wings wrapped around his legs. He gulped, his mouth dry as desert sand. The look on his father's face turned thunderous.

"He named it?" Da spat, turning on Robby. "What were you thinking? How could you let your brother bring home another mouth? One we can ill afford to feed. And you let him name it?"

Robby shifted uncomfortably. He glanced at Jackson. "You don't understand, Da. I didn't have a choice."

"Unless that thing flew in through the window, what do you mean you didn't have a choice? I'd wager your brother didn't lift it into the truck alone." Cullum angrily dragged a hand through his dark hair.

Robby leaned toward their father and lowered his voice. "When you've finished telling Jackson he can't keep it, let me know what you want me to do. In the meantime, I'll be unloading the feed into the freezers."

Jackson laid a protective hand on the trembling dragonet. Tivet snaked his head under Jackson's arm, resting his snout against the boy's bony chest.

The same compulsion, the one that led Jackson to the back of the Travellers' caravan in the first place, reasserted itself. He looked down. The dragonet's gaze locked with his, and it was as if something missing finally clicked into place.

~Mine, a wispy voice sounded in Jackson's mind. His knees weakened at the alien voice in his head.

~Tivet? Jackson responded.

Cullum McLoughlin considered the pair and quickly

concluded he'd never seen a more pathetic duo. He loved his fragile son just as much as his other three boys. Yet, he had to admit there was a special place in his heart for this child. That didn't mean Cullum didn't recognize the vast differences between the three older siblings and Jackson. And as much as Cullum would have wished otherwise, allowances had to be made for Jackson's *limitations*.

Dragon Speakers were born, not taught. In the long line of McLoughlin's, no child had ever been born creature deaf—that is, until Jackson came along. There was no way around it. You couldn't handle a dragon if you couldn't communicate with it on a subliminal level. That left only scut work for Jackson—cleaning stalls and throwing feed to only the gentlest of the dragons.

Why Jackson couldn't communicate with dragons was a mystery, one the entire family had yet to unravel.

From his first breath on this earth, Cullum recognized this son had been different from his others. Jackson didn't come screaming into the world as his brothers had. Nor did Jackson share their dark blue eyes and black hair. And as the years passed, Cullum wasn't blind to the fact that it wasn't the differences in their physical traits that bothered his diminutive son. Without question, being creature deaf was what bedeviled Jackson the most. And no matter what anybody said or how much love they heaped upon his delicate frame, Jackson didn't change. He seldom smiled and never succumbed to intense displays of emotion.

"You can't keep him, Jack." Cullum felt sick, even as the words left his mouth. While the stricken look on Jackson's face was unsurprising, the words that spilled from the boy's mouth left Cullum speechless.

"I can, and I will." Jackson clutched the small dragonet's head to his chest. "And if you try to take him, I will hate you forever!"

What the . . . Cullum grimaced as Jackson burst into tears, fell to his knees, and buried his face against the sickly dragonet.

"What's going on here?" As was usually the case, Cullum hadn't heard his wife's approach. "Heaven help us." She rushed to wrap her arms around the frightened pair. "What have you done, Cullum?" Lorelei pierced her husband with *the* stare, the one only she could pull off. Resigned, he watched her lovingly stroking their son's springy ginger curls. "It's okay, my heart. Whatever it is, we'll fix it."

"I just told him he couldn't keep that thing." Cullum had to try, even though he knew he'd already lost. "You know we can't, Lorelei."

Lorelei pulled back and took a good look at the sad little dragonet. "Cullum, it's just a baby. I don't see why Jack can't keep him."

"Because it won't always be a baby, and we can't afford the responsibility of another worthless piece of baggage."

"Like me?" Jackson raised his tear-stained face.

Cullum rocked back on his heels. The hits just kept coming. *Is that what he thinks?* Cullum's eyes widened as he turned his troubled gaze on his wife.

"Let him keep him," she mouthed.

At that point, backed into a corner, he sighed, and any residual resistance quickly evaporated. After all these years, he'd better know what was good for him.

"All right, Jack. You can keep him . . . for now." Cullum frowned at the dried-up husk Jackson clutched so tightly. "But caring for Tivet is your responsibility—no one else's. I don't want to see him running around underfoot. No slacking off on your chores. And," Cullum ticked off each demand on his callused fingers, "there'd better not be any falling behind on your schoolwork either."

"We won't let you down, Da. I promise." Jackson's eyes brightened with a glimmer of newfound hope.

We? Cullum thought as he cocked an eyebrow at his wife. She shrugged, a small smile flirting at the corners of her mouth.

"All right then, put Tivet in the quarantine barn. He looks like a walking infection. I'll meet you there after I've fixed him something to eat. Though I dare say it won't be much. Otherwise, it'll just make him sick."

Cullum watched Jackson disentangle himself from the clingy dragonet and lead him away—his overly long wings leaving a distinctive trail in the dirt.

"You did the right thing, my love."

"I don't know. Something doesn't feel right about this." He wrapped his arm around her waist. "We'll get the truth out of Robby. He was there. Loaded the darn thing in the truck, mind you."

"Whatever the consequences, we'll deal with it as a family." She rested her head against his shoulder. "You realize our son just threw his first tantrum?"

"Yeah, I do." Cullum's chiseled features broke into a toothy grin. "Ain't it grand, though."

CHAPTER SIX

JACKSON SCATTERED THE TIMOTHY hay around the center of the enclosure, building up the edges as he went. There was no sense in bedding down an entire quarantine stall built to house dragons with massive wingspans. Tivet was only a tiny thing, after all.

"That ought to do it." Jackson looked at Tivet, who stood beyond the stall's entrance as he watched Jackson work. "You want to try out your new nest?"

~No. Tivet dropped to the ground and closed his eyes, his head resting on his front legs.

His resounding no startled Jackson. He was still reeling from the first sounds Tivet had made in his head. *Me, Jackson the Deaf, the scourge of our family tree, can hear a dragon?* He paused at the thought, which led him to another. *I wonder if I can talk to all dragons?*

~No.

"Hey, you shouldn't listen to my private thoughts."

~*If you don't want me to hear your thoughts, your thoughts shouldn't be so loud.*

"Can I think quietly?"

~Can you?

"How would I know if I can think in any other way than how I already do?" Jackson shrugged and continued. "Besides, my whole life has been a mistake. My parents didn't want me. My brothers think I'm flawed. I haven't had any training because there was nothing to train. Maybe now that I can hear you, Da can help me learn."

~No. You mustn't tell anyone. Tivet sat up, whipping his tail back and forth in the dust.

"Why ever not?" Jackson lifted his hands. "All my life, I've thought I was broken, not good enough, and now that I know that's not true, why wouldn't I tell my folks?"

~Once spoken, it can never be unsaid.

"Why would they care? My entire family are Dragon Speakers. They'll want to talk to you."

~No. They won't.

"Because you won't talk to them?"

~Even if I did, they wouldn't hear me. Until you, no one ever has.

Jackson frowned as he considered the dragonet. "That's strange. Can you talk to other dragons?

~I've never met any.

"Never?"

~Never.

"Well, I guess there's no hurry. But eventually, they'll have to know I can hear you."

~Maybe.

"What's that supposed to mean?" Jackson waited, but Tivet didn't respond. "Aren't you going to come and try out your new bed?"

~No.

"Why not? Is something wrong with it? It seems you won't know until you've given it a go."

Tivet raised his head and looked at the iron door rolled to

one side. ~*Cage.*

"This is not a cage." Jackson waived his arms at the cave-like enclosure, with its mud-daubed walls and earthen floor. A feeding pedestal stood within easy reach of the gate, and water trickled into a large trough nearby. "It's a dragon lair and a nice one if I do say so myself. I helped build it."

~*Iron bars. It's a prison.*

"Tivet, my da would never allow me to leave the gates open."

~*If I won't stay in your prison, will you make me leave?* He curled in on himself, and his tiny body began to shake.

Jackson closed the distance between them. Leaning over, he lifted Tivet's black snout and looked into his slit pupils, which whorled with color. "I will never make you leave. If you go, I go with you."

Tivet inhaled deeply. ~*Your words smell true.*

"You can tell when people lie?" Jackson lowered himself to sit cross-legged before his new friend.

~*Impure intentions smell the same as lies. There were a lot of both with the Travellers. Besides, I learned to understand what they were saying to each other. Mostly, I only bothered to listen when they talked about me.*

"How did you come to be with them? In fact, where did you come from? Where were you hatched?"

~*I don't know where they found my egg. But I was hatched in their campfire two winters past.*

"You're two years old? But you're so small."

~*Do you think that's why the kids taunted me? Because I don't look right?*

"I don't know." Jackson scooted closer and wrapped his arms around the little dragonet.

~*The night before you came, I heard the men laughing around the campfire. They said it had been a long time since they'd tasted dragon meat.* His ocean-blue eyes darkened.

~They weren't going to stop with a beating the next time.

"Tivet, I swear I will stand between you and anyone who wants to hurt you."

CHAPTER SEVEN

CULLUM FOUND JACKSON SEATED on the ground with his arms wrapped around the small dragonet. While not unsurprising, what gave Cullum pause was the deep sorrow etched into his son's features. *Maybe this isn't such a good idea after all.*

"Jackson, why is your charge not in his enclosure?" Closing the distance, he tried to sound as normal as possible. Still, he couldn't ignore what he was seeing.

Startled, Jackson jumped up and rubbed his shirt sleeve over his eyes. "Uh . . . I just finished laying the bedding. I was resting."

"Resting. Is that what you were doing?" Cullum cocked a bushy brow. "Well, come on, let's get Tivet settled inside. The vet is on his way. We can't treat this little tike differently than any other dragon introduced into our racing stable." Cullum held out a metal bowl. "Here's his first meal."

⬦⬦⬦⬦

JACKSON TOOK THE BOWL, noting it contained barely a pound of meat and didn't resemble what they fed the other dragons.

Grayish and lumpy, it appeared rather unappetizing.

"That's it?"

"For now, but take a good look at him." Cullum indicated the dragonet at their feet. "He's malnourished to the point that his scales are dried out and cracking. I'm surprised he hasn't shed them. If we give him too much rich feed, he'll get colic. Need I remind you what happens when a dragon gets colic?"

"No, sir." Jackson sniffed at the bowl's gelatinous contents. "What's in this?"

"Ground lamb, eggs, and powdered goats' milk."

"And oatmeal to make it stick together," Jackson added.

"That's right. Do you recognize anything else?"

Jackson took another whiff. "Brewer's yeast?"

"And why would I include that in the mixture?" Cullum quizzed.

Jackson took in Tivet's sad state. He was matte black all over, and instead of a series of sleek and shiny overlapping scales, not only were they cracked, but they were also strangely curled along the edges.

"It will stabilize his digestion if his bowels get loose, and it'll help repair his scales."

~*What do you think? Do you want to give it a try?* Jackson held the bowl under the dragonet's snout.

Using his foreleg, Tivet covered his nostrils.

"Those are just a few benefits from a regular dose of Brewer's yeast." Cullum moved to inspect the enclosure and added over his shoulder. "I've put Tivet on the feeding chart. I want it followed carefully. Instead of twice a day like the other dragons, you'll feed him four times a day at six-hour intervals. Now, how about we get him settled before Doc gets here."

Jackson picked up Tivet's lead rope and started into the stall. The tiny dragonet leaned back, his claws digging into the shed row's packed earth.

Cullum put his hands on his hips, a frown forming. "I

suppose we shouldn't be surprised that we'll have to teach him some manners."

"No, Da. He's afraid of the gates. He must think this is a cage."

"We can't have him running loose around the compound. He's not a dog, and there's a reason we have quarantine procedures. I can't jeopardize our other dragons when introducing a new one, especially one we know nothing about or where he originally came from. It's obvious he wasn't well cared for."

"The Travellers were going to kill him tonight."

~No! You mustn't give us away.

"And how would you know that?" His father asked.

"Uh . . . those Traveller kids were beating him with wooden swords. Why else would they be allowed to do that?"

"Savages," Cullum growled.

"Is this my new patient?" Doc Miller had arrived. "Wow! I'd say we have our work cut out for us. Where'd you get this one, Cullum? The dragon slag heap?"

CHAPTER EIGHT

THOUGH HE UNDERSTOOD DOC WAS trying TO be funny, Jackson couldn't help feeling peeved over the slag heap remark. He hadn't found Doc Miller prone to unkind comments in the past. Generally, unless immersed in stabilizing an injured dragon, he was one of those upbeat guys that people liked to be around.

Doc set his bag down and squatted to get a better look at Tivet. He stroked the cowering dragonet a few times before gently grasping the tip of one wing. Rising, he unfurled the wing to its full length, inspecting both sides of the appendage, paying particular attention to where the wing attached to the shoulder.

"You ever see anything like this, Cullum?"

"No, I can't say that I have. Is it a deformity?"

"It doesn't look like it. I think it's just the way he's made." Refolding the wing, Doc repeated the process on the other side. "Identical. It's almost as if his wing joints are hypermobile. How old is this little guy?"

Cullum straightened and looked to his son for the answer.

"I don't know." Jackson shrugged. "Though as I led Tivet

back through the camp, I overheard a couple of older Travellers talking about two years wasted. They might have been referring to Tivet. Besides, once the deal had been struck, they weren't interested in talking, at least not to me."

"Travellers? You don't say?" Doc looked appalled. "Travellers with a live dragon?" He lifted his plaid paddy cap, scratched his bald pate, and regarded Jackson. "I'd be guessing you've got an interesting story to tell."

"I'm sure he does," Cullum commented dryly. "But we haven't gotten around to hearing it yet. Jack will have some explaining to do once we've finished here. So, what's the verdict, Doc?"

"Well." He resettled his cap. "Except for the wings, I'd say he's the size of a six-month-old dragonet." Doc rubbed his chin as he watched Tivet bury his snout beneath his wing. "However, the wing ratio to body height and length is more like what you'd find on a far older dragonet than six months. Can he fly?"

"I wouldn't think so. He's too malnourished to have the strength needed for lift-off. And from what Jackson *has* told me," His da paused long enough to give him the hairy eyeball, "they probably kept him tied up, and Jack thinks they were planning on eating the pitiful thing."

"Eat a dragon?" If possible, Doc appeared even more disturbed at this revelation. "Who does that sort of thing?"

"Come on, Doc. You can't be that naïve. Some people will eat anything if they're hungry enough." Cullum pointed at the skeletal creature. "But I don't see enough meat on that frame to nourish a starving dog, let alone a family. I suspect we've got a clan of dragon haters on our hands. And they'd like nothing more than to eat the object of their loathing."

"Dragon haters? Haven't seen any of those for a decade or more." Doc observed.

"At least," Cullum muttered under his breath. "We sure

don't need their kind around here. Not right now." He looked off into the distance, the lines bracketing his mouth deepening. "Not ever."

"What's a dragon hater?" Jackson looked between the two men.

Cullum considered his answer before he began to speak. "Before my father's time and before his and his father's time, life was far harsher than it is today. One of the things they had to deal with was a land where dragons roamed free, and they were worse than wolves when it came to killing livestock. One dragon line was said to be particularly good at decimating entire herds in the far northern countries—Icelandic Sleek Backed Swifts. The locals called them Death Spooks."

A ray of late afternoon sunshine pierced the gathering gloom through the stall's window. The dust motes that rode the air drew Jackson's attention as he listened to his father's story. "And as the legend goes, after the Swifts migrated to Northern Ireland, the people who suffered the most from Death Spooks were the hardiest folk, those who populated the northernmost counties. Due to the Spooks' coloring and swiftness, they cleaned out most of the wildlife over the span of a single winter."

Jackson's eyes widened. He'd never heard this story before. "What did they look like?"

"Again, according to legend, Death Spooks were ghostly—mostly the color of winter cloud cover. However, like chameleons, they could change their coloring with the shifting skies. In appearance, they also differed from other dragon species in that they were smaller, sleeker, faster, and more maneuverable. All of this made for a perfect ambush predator." Cullum waved his fingers, disrupting the particles of dust. "By the time you spotted one, it was too late."

A shiver passed through Jackson as he imagined a harbinger of death as nothing more than a shadow on the ground. No time to react. No time to pray.

"Once the livestock was gone and the woodlands stripped of game, the clans faced starvation. They had no choice but to abandon everything they had worked so hard for and take to the road. But there was one thing they didn't leave behind." Cullum paused; a flick of sorrow crossed his features. "Hearts filled with hatred and an unquenchable thirst for vengeance."

"I mean, who would blame them?" Jackson couldn't help but feel sympathy for those who had lived and died so long ago. Forced from their homes by a menace they had no hope to stand against.

"Vengeance is never an answer, Jack," His da said before he continued the tale. "Years passed, and the clans embraced their nomadic lifestyle. Eradicating dragons became an integral part of their new culture." His fist clenched, Cullum strode into the stall and stopped before the window to frown at the sky. His robust features were etched in sunlight as his tone turned dark, gravelly.

"Instead of leaving the carcasses to rot, generations of Travellers made a living by selling dragon body parts. Dragon scales, in particular, were in high demand. As you can imagine, they were useful for many things, including armor. Also, they uncovered a ready market with the practitioners of ancient folk medicine, those who believed specific dragon organs could cure various human ailments. And what the Travellers didn't sell, they ate. The hunters thrived off the slaughter, and as weapons improved, they got so good they threatened the very existence of all the dragon species.

"It wasn't until only a small number of dragons remained that the government finally put a stop to the wholesale slaughter. By adding them to the worldwide endangered species list, killing and trading in dragon parts became a felony. With the ending of the illegal trading, the intent was to allow the dragon populations to recover and avoid the specter of extinction. But it was too late for the species who'd spawned the dragon hunters. Death Spooks have not been seen for over two hundred years, besides the occasional unearthed skeletal remains." Cullum stared into the distance for several seconds before he shook himself, returning his gaze to Jackson.

"I suppose the Travellers you met today could be direct descendants of the original clans. And if we have dragon haters in the area, we must be alert and warn all the farms to be extra cautious."

"Particularly when they're working their stock," Doc said. "I treated a dragon over at the Frazer's the other day. It had a tear in its wing that Johnny was sure hadn't been there when he took him out for flight training. Now that I think about it, a Broadhead arrow could have caused that wound."

~Your da's right. I could hear them talking at night. They hate dragons and the people who raise them even more.

"What are we going to do?" Jackson asked his da.

"Well, for now, we can do nothing without proof, " Cullum said, looking at Tivet. "Mistreating one dragonet isn't enough to point the finger at the whole lot of them. Not all Travellers are dragon haters.

"Anyway, storytime's over. Let's finish giving Tivet the once over, and then we should get the word out to the other farms." Cullum pointed at the bedding. "Jack, why don't you move him over there so Doc can get a better look at him."

Jackson tugged on the rope. Tivet responded by sitting back on his haunches and digging his claws into the dirt.

~ Don't do this. Not now. Not in front of my da. If you're allowed to stay here, we must follow the rules.

Tivet lowered his head until it barely cleared the ground. He slunk forward one hesitant step at a time, his long tail and wingtips leaving a fresh set of furrows in his wake.

"Well, I can't say I like the looks of that." Doc picked up his bag and followed them into the enclosure.

CHAPTER NINE

JACKSON SETTLED THE FOOD dish beside the dragonet and stepped back to watch. Tivet took one sniff, turned his back, and dropped to his belly. Curling in on himself, he wrapped his tail and its jagged tip tightly around his body.

Jackson pushed the dish a bit closer. Tivet responded by tucking his head further under his wing.

"See if you can get him to stand, Jack," Cullum said.

"That's okay. Tivet's fine where he is. Though I haven't been able to communicate with him." Doc, a Dragon Speaker himself, had every reason to be suspicious. "Does he bite? Or, more importantly, does he flame?"

~I won't hurt him.

"He won't hurt you, Doc," Jackson said.

"You don't know that," his da shot back. "Why don't you grab a small muzzle? It'll be too big, but it'll be better than nothing."

"He didn't hurt any of those kids who were trying to kill him, and he had every right."

"Maybe so, but we would be foolish to take a chance with a dragonet we know nothing about."

"Leave it. He seems gentle enough." Doc settled on his knees next to Jackson and the dragonet. "The shape he's in, I'm not sure he could generate enough flame to spark a match."

"If you're sure." Cullum stepped closer.

"So, little guy, what's going on with you?" Doc ran his hands over Tivet's scales and began to pick along the edges, peering underneath several. "I don't know how you've managed to survive as long as you have, mister." Doc poked and prodded until he came to Tivet's head. Inserting a finger along the outside edge of his maw, Doc encouraged the dragonet to open up. After a few minutes, the vet sat back and reached inside his bag, pulling out what was needed to draw a blood sample.

"This might pinch a little. You want to hold his head, Jackson?" Doc directed.

~I already said I wouldn't bite him.

~I know. But I can't tell him what you said to me, now can I? Jackson responded in mind-speak.

~True.

Jackson rubbed the dragonet's tiny horn buds as Doc inserted the needle under a scale and drew the blood.

"Can you get him to roll over so I can listen to what's happening inside his chest?" Doc carefully put the blood sample into one of several side pockets in his medical bag, then pulled out a stethoscope.

Tivet's body went rigid.

~Come on, you can do this. Jackson scratched under Tivet's chin with one hand as he encouraged him to roll onto his side.

The little dragonet began to tremble. Baring his vulnerable underbelly would take a leap of faith, the type of trust Jackson wasn't sure the abused juvenile had left to give.

"Here, let me." Cullum crouched, prepared to help wrestle

Tivet onto his side.

"No! Don't touch him," Jackson snapped, impulsively pushing his father's hands away.

"Jack . . ." Cullum's tone wasn't the kind that Jackson could ignore.

"Please, Da, he's scared. Those awful people tortured him, and who knows for how long." While he knew it had been for the entire two years of Tivet's life, it was just another thing Jackson shouldn't have known about. "Just give me a second."

"All right, let's see if you're a better dragon whisperer than I."

It was at that moment Jackson realized his da may have been trying to communicate with Tivet without success.

~I don't think he can. I haven't heard anything other than what comes out of his mouth. You're the only human I've ever been able to talk with. While I learned to understand what the Travellers were saying among themselves, it was never in my head. But this, between us? I didn't know hearing another's thoughts inside my head was possible.

~It's not possible. My da told me that dragons don't understand spoken language, only the unspoken language of intent. Dragon Speakers imagine what they want, and their dragons learn to comply. And that's when the second metaphorical shoe landed. He'd been communicating to Tivet for the last couple of hours, and not once had it occurred to Jackson how far outside the norm it was. Utterly different from everything he had learned about dragon speaking and how it worked. What he and Tivet had been doing together came to him as naturally as breathing.

"Jack . . ." Cullum cleared his throat. "We're waiting."

~I will be right here the whole time, Tivet. If you can trust me, even a little, hear me when I say Doc would never hurt you. I'll admit that sometimes the treatments can be uncomfortable, but they're intended to help, not hurt. I

promise I'll keep my hand right next to his.

With one last shudder, Tivet rolled to his side, exposing his pale underbelly.

CHAPTER TEN

WITH THE EXAMINATION COMPLETE AND the dragonet's head settled on his lap, Jackson struggled to rein in his impatience. He needed to know that his new friend was going to be alright.

Doc scrubbed his hands with alcohol before he closed his medical bag and gave them his opinion.

"Well, I don't have to tell you he's malnourished. And I wouldn't go wrong wagering that he's been suffering since he was hatched. Whether somebody intentionally mistreated him, or he has some underlying condition that keeps his body from absorbing the nutrition he needs." Doc lifted his hands. "Who's to say? We're not going to be getting any answers from the Travellers."

"Is he going to be all right?" Jackson's concern grew with each sentence Doc uttered.

"We'll know more in a few days after I've received the test results." Doc frowned in thought. "I don't think his life is in danger, Jack. But . . . and that's a big but, I don't know if Tivet will ever completely recover and be what he could have been with a better start in life."

"What do you mean by that?" Jackson's heart sped up.

"This is no newborn. And as I've said, the wing-to-body height and length ratio is what we would find in a much older dragon. Maybe as many as ten years. His teeth aren't giving me a lot of insight, either. So, whether he was born stunted or with a defective immune system that has kept him from thriving, we'll never know for sure." Doc bent over and knuckled Tivet's head. "He's a cute little thing. Interesting eye color. I've not seen the like. But then, I haven't treated a dragon like him before."

~Doc says you could be ten years old, and he thinks you're stunted, making you appear much younger. But you said you hatched two years ago.

~I was. He doesn't know what he's talking about.

"I'm going to run some genetic tests on the blood sample, which might give us insight into his past." Straightening, Doc faced Cullum. "There's a lot for us to unpack here. In the meantime, be very cautious with this guy. He's literally on the ragged edge. He's far too cold and not generating enough heat on his own. And his heart rate is too slow, especially considering his size.

"He has no body fat and little in the way of muscle tone. The condition of the scales is the most obvious indication of his overall health. Dull and brittle, they've curled up on the edges. I've never seen scales this damaged that hadn't already sloughed off."

"Anything we can do topically?" Cullum asked.

"Jack could give him a good lanolin rubdown each day, and even with that, I'm not sure it'll prevent him from losing those scales." Doc paused and exchanged a long look with Cullum. "I don't need to tell you how dangerous losing his scales would be in his current condition. Still, let's not borrow more trouble than we already have. We'll deal with it when and if it happens."

~I'll take care of you, don't worry. Jackson stroked Tivet's

triangular-shaped head.

"I'll need a stool sample to check for worms, so you'll have to do that once there's something to collect. None of us wants to do a rectal exam on a dragon, no matter how small. I'll leave you a deworming tonic but don't use it until we know if he's infested and how badly. If we dose him before we know, a big parasite die-off could poison his blood and kill him, particularly if he has blood worms. A die-off of that magnitude and the toxicity it caused would undoubtedly stop his heart."

"Is that it?" Cullum huffed, shaking his head.

"As you're aware, given his condition, it would be prudent to increase his food intake slowly over the next few days. Though it doesn't look like overeating will be a problem over the long haul." Doc eyeballed the untouched feed. "You might try some ground chicken instead of the lamb. You know how dragons like chicken? It might spark his appetite."

"You don't think he's infectious?" Cullum asked.

"I don't think so, but again, I can't be sure. I'm going to run a full diagnostic panel. That should rule out the worst things that would likely keep us up at night. I'll have most of the results for you by tomorrow. The genetic test will take a lot longer. To be safe, you might want to keep him in the quarantine barn until further notice."

"That goes without saying." Cullum turned his gaze on Jackson. "We on the same page, Jack?"

"Yes, sir."

Doc laughed, then looked at the pathetic lump amid the sage-colored bedding. "Jackson, I think the best medicine right now is to show Tivet a gentle hand. It would appear he's experienced very little other than the stick."

"No, I don't think he has," Jackson whispered.

CHAPTER ELEVEN

TWILIGHT WAS WELL UPON THEM when Jackson watched his father and the vet leave the barn.

"You want to eat this?" Jackson held the feed bowl under Tivet's snout. With no one around, Jackson spoke his words aloud.

~*I'm not hungry.*

"You need to eat." Jackson scooped a bit of the beige-colored mash onto the tip of his finger. "Why not see what it tastes like? You might like it."

Tivet's nostrils flared. ~*It doesn't smell right.*

"What do you mean it doesn't smell right?" Jackson sniffed the offering. "Smells all right to me."

~*Then you eat it—no sense in letting it go to waste. Nothing went to waste in camp. They fed me what nobody else would touch, when I was fed at all. Rotten garbage and this smells just like it.*

"I don't see how this could smell worse than rotting garbage. Besides, it's raw. I can't eat raw meat."

~*And I should?* Tivet tipped his head.

"That's what dragons eat, mostly. If I cook it, will you eat then?"

~*Maybe.*

"Maybe?" Jackson sighed. "What *do* you like to eat?"

~Nothing. I told you already. I didn't get what was left over after they'd finished eating. No, it was nasty before they threw it my way. I only choked down enough to survive. Every day seemed worse than the last. Tivet lowered his head into the Timothy. *~I don't know why I even tried.*

"Because you didn't know anything else." Jackson's chest grew heavy at Tivet's revelations. The things he'd endured from the moment he'd been hatched. For a baby to never know a day without hunger, nor a day without fear, broke Jackson's heart.

"I tell you what, since I already have this on my finger, stick your tongue out and clean it off for me. I'll heat a new batch on the stove." Jackson rested his finger on Tivet's lips. When he refused to open his mouth, Jackson smeared the gelatinous goop along the seam where Tivet pressed his lips together.

"I'll be right back." Jackson glanced at the gates and set the bowl down. "If I leave the gate open, promise me you won't leave. If my da found you wandering outside, I'd get in heaps of trouble."

~I trusted you, and you haven't violated that trust. So why won't you trust me?

"Okay. I trust you to stay here." Jackson nodded and left the stall but didn't go far. Standing in the shadows, he watched as the little dragonet rubbed his snout back and forth in the bedding. When that failed to rid him of the sticky mash, he tried dragging a front leg over it, transferring the feed to his foreleg. Tivet sniffed at the mess he'd made, curled his lip, and circled through the bedding several times before settling. Resting his head between his legs, he closed his eyes only to reopen them. With his nostrils pinched, he glared at the offensive mass.

Jackson covered his mouth and tried to hold back his

laughter at the dragonet's fit of pure contrariness.

Emitting a low growl, Tivet pushed at the gunk with his tongue. His eyes widened, and he rubbed his lips together. A series of enthusiastic licks later, and Tivet's forearm was clean.

Smacking his lips, he peered around. Satisfied he wasn't being observed, Tivet crept toward the bowl. Lowering his head, he took one last sniff before his snout disappeared over the edge. Jackson grinned as he watched the ornery little dragonet gobble up the contents and lick the bowl before flipping it over to snuffle greedily through the bedding, searching for any dregs he may have missed.

Delighted, Jackson hurried away. He still had to help his brothers with the evening chores and was already late.

Chapter Twelve

DEEP IN THOUGHT, CULLUM PERUSED the daily training chart for the month ahead. Blotter-sized, it had room to list twenty dragons down the left side and enough boxes to the right to cover as many as thirty-one days in a month. Charts were a trainer's bible of a sort, where he both plotted and noted daily training activities for each dragon under his care.

Cullum placed notations next to each dragon's name using a lead pencil with an erasure tip. As he finished his second cup of coffee, he paused to consider the column of names. Far too many were lined through with the date the dragon had shipped out, and the last three months had been particularly concerning. That their training barn was far from full bothered him greatly. He could no longer ignore the steady drop in the farm's income. If the current trend continued, things would become dire.

Closing his eyes, Cullum pinched the bridge of his nose between his thumb and forefinger. The really troubling part? There was nothing he could do about it. There'd always been a friendly competition between the local trainers to acquire and retain quality bloodstock and the clients who came with them, those who paid their training bills on time. However, anything gentlemanly about the local game ended when Duffy Nolan, the big player on the European circuit, swooped in and started buying up land. And he didn't stop there. Nolan's latest gambit involved buying the best local racing dragons and breeding stock.

If that weren't enough, he'd delivered the killing blow to the local trainers by bringing in his second-string flyers from the more challenging European circuit. Duffy Nolan was close to dominating the local racing scene. With each win his dragons notched, more dragon owners jumped ship, eager to get their flyers into Nolan's stable, hoping to increase their odds of winning. Everybody loved a winner.

As if that would make a difference. Nolan's dragons were just that much better, and the man didn't care what it took to come out on top. Though there was nothing he could prove, Cullum smelled a fox in the henhouse. Things were going far too well for Nolan. Nobody was that lucky.

Cullum's pencil came to rest between two names on the chart—Luna and Nightwing. Both dragons belonged to Regan Malony—McLoughlin Farms' last and most loyal client. Cullum's eyes followed the blank line across the page to where he'd penciled RD. Race Day. The culmination of years of effort. Luna and Nightwing had been hatched and raised on the farm, and brother and sister were sold to Regan as racing prospects. And next to Nocturne, McLoughlin Farms' long-time star, those were two of the best the farm had ever produced. They should win against whatever Nolan trotted out. *Should? Would!*

Feeling grumpy, Cullum set the pencil down, got up, and crossed the hall connecting his office to the sprawling farmhouse kitchen. Refilling his cup, he turned and leaned against the counter, watching Lorelei gather ingredients for breakfast. Today, she wore her favorite stonewashed blue jeans and a pink hand-knitted Aran jumper; his heart swelled, clogging his throat. The love of his life was a sight to watch, bustling and humming her favorite Celtic tune. If he stayed quiet long enough, she might even break into song.

The dark green enameled Aga expelled heat into the room, and the yeasty smell of biscuits already filled the air. The atmosphere of love that Lorelei's kitchen pumped out worked its magic. Cullum relaxed as he felt his angst unravel bit by bit.

"Have you seen our youngest yet?" He lifted his cup and sipped the dark brew. "He's usually up before his brothers."

"He's not in his bed." Lorelei cracked eggs into a crockery mixing bowl.

"No? Where is he then?"

"Need you ask?" Lorelei laughed.

"So, he got up early to check on his new charge?" Cullum didn't wait for his wife's response before continuing. "I guess that shouldn't be entirely unexpected, especially after the way he carried on yesterday."

"His bed hasn't been slept in."

"He slept with that runt?" Cullum couldn't hide his shock.

"You, of all people, shouldn't be so surprised. You've slept next to a few critters over the years." Lorelei began whisking the eggs, adding a dash of salt and pepper and a dollop of buttermilk. "And they weren't all dragons."

"Not next to, nearby. Besides, that only happened when the situation was dire."

"Maybe so, but keep in mind this is the first dragon Jack has been allowed to take a real interest in. Sure, he cares for all the dragons, they're part of his daily chores, but since he's creature deaf, he's always felt left out." She held up her hand before Cullum could protest. "I know. We've all tried to convince him otherwise. But we've had to treat him differently since he couldn't communicate with the dragons. You can't deny it. While it was the only way to protect him, he didn't see it that way.

"I know we didn't talk about what happened yesterday," Lorelei continued. "But I think we both got the message about how strongly our son feels about his disability. He thinks he's a burden to the family."

"I . . . well . . ." Cullum dragged his hand through his hair. "What are we going to do?"

"We're going to let him keep the dragonet while we encourage him in every way possible." Lorelei cocked her head, listening to the noises coming from the second floor. "I think the rest of your brawny brood have smelled the biscuits."

"My brood, huh?" Cullum put his cup down and crossed over to wrap his arms around his wife's waist as she poured the egg mixture into a hot skillet heating on the Aga's front burner. "More like spawn, and as I recall, you had a part to play."

Setting the empty bowl aside, Lorelei turned within the circle of his arms. "Aye, and I'd gladly do it all again." She wrapped her arms around his neck and leaned in for the kiss he offered.

"Hey, you two need to knock that off." Aidan laughed as he strode into the kitchen. "And right now, before the eggs get burnt."

"Burnt eggs, you say? What a way to ruin a perfectly good morning." Brandon pushed past his brother. "Who's responsible for this tragedy? Oh . . . I see."

Cullum finished their leisurely kiss before letting Lorelei push him away. Returning her attention to the egg mixture, she added crumbled cheese.

"Every good cook needs to be shown a proper amount of appreciation," Cullum smirked. "You boys should be thanking me."

Lorelei snorted.

"What's all this about burnt eggs?" Robby shouted from the stairs.

"Oh, for heaven's sake, the eggs are not burned, but they will be if all of you don't give it a break." Lorelei wasn't unfamiliar with their good-natured teasing. "Set the table."

"Where's our favorite little red-headed munchkin?" Aidan hugged his mum and gently tugged her silver-gray braid. "Robby tells us that Jack's had a dragonet follow him home." Aidan grabbed the silverware as Brandon filled the coffee mugs.

"Not exactly the words I used." Robby got Brandon in a headlock and gave him a noogie.

"Hey, watch it, Robby. You make me spill the coffee, and it'll be your cup that ends up empty."

"Jack slept in the barn with Tivet." Cullum filled in his sons.

"He named it?" Aidan gasped in an overly dramatic tone.

"That's what I said." Cullum glanced over at his wife, who gave him the stink eye as she pulled a tray of hot biscuits from the oven. Taking the hint, he toned it down before continuing. "But . . . it's important that we don't tease him about this. He was pretty upset yesterday. Your mum and I have decided that since this is the first dragon Jack has taken an interest in, it will be a valuable learning opportunity. And maybe not just for Jack, either."

"I'm warning you hyenas, if you don't show some restraint and start showing compassion for your brother's sensitivity over his creature deafness . . ." Lorelei cast a stern look around. "I will have to get involved." She set the rest of the food in the center of the table. "Have I made myself clear enough?"

Three brawny lads exchanged glances and nodded as a unit.

"He's our brother, Mama Bear." Aiden got up and wrapped his arms around his mother. "We all love him. Not one of us would refuse to lay our lives down for any member of this family," he said, his face serious. "But that little peanut is number one in my book. So, where's his share of this feast? I'll take it to him."

CHAPTER THIRTEEN

AIDEN CONSIDERED HIMSELF TO BE pretty resilient. But finding his little brother draped in a dark dragonet wing and snoring softly in a bed of Timothy, nearly did him in.

A shaft of the early morning sun speared through the enclosure's window, bathing the dynamic duo in its golden rays. Jackson's body was turned toward the dragonet. Tivet's long neck curled protectively around Jackson's head. The latter's thatch of fiery red curls ruffled with each of the dragonet's exhalations.

Aiden wished he'd thought to bring his cell phone. Knowing his mother, she would have cherished a picture of this little scene. There was always room for another photo in the family album. He snorted softly to himself. No, this scene would have been blown up, framed, and taken center stage in the family gallery.

He shook himself from his reverie. Jackson's breakfast wasn't getting any warmer. Stepping into the stall, Aiden touched his brother's shoulder, freezing when the dragonet's eyes opened. Like a snake, the sleek head lifted, and the swirling ocean-blue eyes turned stormy.

Well-versed in dragon body language, Aiden knew what he faced. The tiny creature, by dragon standards, didn't pose a real threat unless he flamed him. However, that appeared unlikely with Jackson in the way. Nonetheless, the dragonet was capable of doling out a nasty bite, and the vibe coming off him was one filled with hostility.

"Okay, little guy, I'm not here to hurt anybody." Even though he knew the dragonet couldn't understand his words, Aiden modulated his tone. At the same time, he tried to connect with the dragonet's mind. But there was nothing. *What the heck?*

"Jack, wake up." Aiden extended his hand toward the creature in a placating gesture. The dragonet hissed. "Jack, you need to wake up. Now."

Jackson stirred. Opening his eyes, he bolted upright. The dragonet unfurled his wings, rising to his feet. Lowering his head, his eyes glowed with malice. It didn't take a mind reader to know what was coming. But when his maw opened, it showcased an astonishingly long set of teeth for such a young dragon, and the sight had Aiden on his heels, backpedaling.

"Whoa, Jack, get control of your dragonet before he does something that can't be undone."

JACKSON SLAPPED HIS HAND over Tivet's muzzle. *~It's my brother. He won't hurt us.*

~Brother? He doesn't look the same as yesterday.

~That was Robby. I have three brothers.

~He should not sneak up on us.

~I don't think he was sneaking. Can you calm down? Jackson could sense the level of Tivet's fear and anxiety. *So, this is what it feels like to be in touch with a dragon's emotions.*

~Yes. And I can feel your fear, too. I won't bite your brother.

~There you go, listening when you shouldn't.

Tivet snorted, slowly relaxing.

Jackson turned to his brother. "This is Tivet. He's a little skittish."

"You could say that again." Aiden held out the covered plate. "I brought your breakfast. You should eat it before it gets cold."

Jackson's stomach gurgled loudly. Sitting cross-legged, he took the proffered plate and peeled back the aluminum foil. A small cloud of steam rose on the cool morning air. The smells that filled his nose made his mouth water. *Eggs, bacon, and buttered biscuits. Yum.*

~What is that? Tivet's head snaked over Jackson's shoulder.

"This is for me, not you." Jackson used his elbow to push Tivet's snout away.

"When's the last time you fed this little guy, Jack."

"Around midnight. Da said to feed him every six hours until he's stronger."

"So, he's not due for another hour." Aiden laughed as Tivet slid his snout under Jackson's arm, trying a different approach to get at the bacon. "You know, if he likes bacon, you might be able to employ it as a training device. He certainly needs it."

"Training device?" Jackson asked around a mouthful of biscuit, a few crumbs falling into the Timothy hay. Following their trajectory, Tivet snuffled loudly through the bedding.

"A reward for good behavior?" Aiden indicated the hungry dragonet eagerly rooting around in the bedding.

"Even though dragons don't understand our spoken language, they're no different than dogs. They can start associating how a specific word sounds with the desired action. Sit, stay, come . . . you know the drill."

"Tivet is a dragon." Jackson stiffened at the perceived slur. "Why would anybody compare him to a dog? He is not a dog!"

"No, he's not." Aiden held up a hand, forestalling further outrage. "I don't need to tell you that dragons are much smarter than dogs, and dogs are pretty darn clever. But let's get real here, Jack. I tried, and he wouldn't respond when he thought about attacking me. We must find another way if he can't or won't use dragon speak. You know he won't always be this small and weak. And it would be far too dangerous to keep a dragon in the barn who can't be taught. Out-of-control dragons are dangerous, Jack. Do you know what would have happened if he'd shown Da that kind of aggression?"

Jackson reeled with the realization of what could have happened.

~Can't you communicate with Aiden if you want to?

~I have no way of knowing and am unwilling to try. I don't trust him.

"You can't communicate with Tivet?" Jackson eyed his brother.

"No. I tried. I've never heard of a dragon that couldn't be reached. While some may not always choose to respond, they can still feel us, and vice versa."

Aiden studied the young dragonet who'd returned to eyeballing Jackson's breakfast and nuzzling his cheek. "Begging? While an annoyance now, what happens when he gets bigger and decides to take what he wants?"

"He won't." Jackson shook his head. "He wouldn't." His voice didn't sound so certain, even to himself.

"You don't know that. It might help if you showed him what behavior you expect from him."

Jackson pushed Tivet away once again and glared at him. *~Are you even paying attention to what my brother is saying? You wouldn't do that to me, would you?*

~I would never hurt you.

~You might not mean to, but you will be bigger than me.

Tivet looked at the food on Jackson's plate before turning away. Curling in on himself, he turned his back to Jackson and Aiden.

"Well, that was unexpected. You give him the hairy eyeball, and he gives up on being a pest?" Aiden raised his eyebrows at his brother. "Something you're not telling me?"

"Of course not. He's probably just tired. And he's not stupid. He's really smart."

"Finish your breakfast, then mix this wee fella some chow. He's hungry." Aiden rose to his full height and ruffled Jackson's hair. "Since you'll be late to start your chores, don't be lollygagging around. I'll cover for you with Da."

"You won't tell Da, will you? He'd take Tivet away from me." Jackson swallowed hard. "Aiden, I can't lose him. I won't."

Aiden's eyes narrowed, and he seemed to consider his words before answering. "I won't tell." He looked at the dragonet and frowned. "For now."

CHAPTER FOURTEEN

WHEN JACKSON ARRIVED AT THE main barn, morning training was already in full swing. Stalls were being mucked out, and two of his brothers were busy setting the riding harnesses on a pair of dragons. Both were on the muscle and anxious to get outside to take flight.

Haltered and clipped to an iron ring, each had its way of showing their impatience as Robby and Brandon moved with quiet efficiency.

Recognizing both dragons, Jackson was careful to stay out of easy reach. Racing dragons were volatile, and receiving an injury wasn't a matter of if but when. Training, experience, and staying alert helped avoid the most severe injuries. Still, they happened and were an accepted part of life for dragon trainers and their families. If you couldn't communicate with the enormous animals, the chance of getting hurt became more likely. And both of these dragons had a bad habit of tormenting Jackson.

Luna, the smaller of the two, was basic brown with burnished copper highlights that kept her from being plain. However, what the young drakaina lacked in eye appeal, she made up for in talent. Nightwing, her brother, on the other hand, inky black and packed with muscle, glistened like polished ebony.

This brother and sister set were the best home-bred racing prospects that had come along for the McLoughlin's in a very long time. Jackson's da had very high expectations. He considered them relatively equal in talent, and as first-time starters, Cullum planned to enter them in the same race. As a team, flying interference and taking turns drafting off each other's tail stream, they'd have a better chance of ending the race in the first and second place finishing positions. Racing strategy was almost as crucial as physical talent and training. But none of that mattered if they didn't have fire in their hearts and the will to win. It was that unbridled determination that marked a genuinely great flyer.

Still, as Jackson let his eye run over the two dragons, he saw it differently from his family. Despite Luna's diminutive size, she had a level of star quality that couldn't be denied. To Jackson, the brown drakaina had always appeared larger than life itself. His gaze was drawn to Luna, no matter who else was around. And as luck would have it, precisely what he'd been trying to avoid occurred. Their gazes locked.

Luna's yellow-orange eyes lit, swirling with mischief. Jackson was already moving when a cloud of bright orange sparks shot from her maw.

"Hey! We'll have none of that now." Brandon nudged Luna with his knee, distracting her. "You know better."

"Luna's feeling feisty today," Jackson muttered, embarrassed as he continued to move further out of range. The sparks wouldn't kill him, but they'd burn holes through his clothes, and it hurt like the dickens before the fiery droplets cooled.

"How is your new charge doing this morning?" Cullum stopped next to Jackson. "Did he eat?"

"He's licking the bowl."

"That's a good sign. Did he keep it all down?" Cullum's gaze strayed to Luna as she continued to act up.

"So far, and he's been whining for more." Jackson followed his father's gaze. "Are Luna and Nightwing gonna be ready by next month?" Jackson might have been leery of the dragons, but that didn't mean he wouldn't recognize when the farm's charges stood a good chance of winning. He was so high on Luna that he planned to break open his piggy bank and place the entirety of its contents wagering on her.

Creature deaf or not, you didn't grow up around a dragon speaking family and not recognize a winner when you saw one. And Jackson was better at it than most. However, he had yet to reveal this talent to his family. What was the point? They wouldn't believe him. He was creature deaf and, as such, good for nothing. His shoulders slumped as he huffed a big sigh.

"What?" His da refocused on him. "Oh. Barring an injury, I don't see why not. And speaking of an injury, I have a challenge in mind for you."

Alarmed, Jackson grew rigid. *Has Aiden reneged on his promise? No, he said he wouldn't tell.*

"Challenge?" Jackson relaxed, perking up. His da never challenged him.

"Yes, one that I think you're perfectly suited for." Cullum started toward the far end of the training barn. "Follow me."

Jackson glanced over his shoulder once more at Luna and Nightwing as he followed his da. Nightwing with his glistening blue-black scales and golden eyes. Luna, symmetrical and perfectly proportioned, moved around like she owned the very air. As she looked back at him, there was a challenge in her eyes. Male dragons were stronger, and under perfect racing conditions, they would have an advantage over the females. *But not you, Luna girl. You're the exception to the rule, aren't you?*

Brandon unhooked her halter from the iron tie ring, and when she dipped her head to take the bridle, her eyes stayed locked with Jackson's.

He didn't need to communicate with her to know what she was planning.

Not today, Luna. Jackson smiled to himself as he made his escape. *Not today.*

CHAPTER FIFTEEN

JACKSON AND HIS FATHER STOOD before what many in the dragon racing community considered the best racing dragon in Ireland and possibly all of Europe.

Jackson's heart filled with sadness as he looked at what had once been a vibrant and beautiful drakaina. Nocturne was lying on her side. She didn't raise her head. Heavily lidded eyes didn't twitch. If he hadn't known better, he would have thought her dead.

At Cullum's touch, she made a half-hearted effort to move her wing, exposing her hind leg and the heinous scar marring its surface. What had once been glistening blue-black scales were replaced with a mottled-gray disfigurement that snaked around to encompass her entire hock. The rope-like scar bulged a full inch above its surroundings. It still looked as painful as the memory of how it came to be.

In her last race, Nocturne, undefeated in her racing career, had flown against Bonescraper in the European Championship Race—The Labyrinth of Ruin. The ultimate winner of this prestigious race would wear the title of Best Racing Dragon of the Year and receive a potful of prize money.

Throughout the three-day race, Nocturne and Bonescraper battled for supremacy—the advantage changing back and forth from one day to the next. At the final mandatory rest stop, opinions among the support personnel were that the competition had come down to a two-dragon race. No one believed any of the other dragons who remained in the grueling competition could overcome the time advantage Bonescraper and Nocturne had built over the previous days of racing.

The smart money had still been on Duffy Nolan's Bonescraper, who was also undefeated, to beat the much smaller Nocturne. But size wasn't the only reason the bookies gave Nolan's dragon short odds. It hadn't been a well-kept secret that Nolan wasn't above using dirty tricks to gain an advantage.

It was dragon racing, after all—a rough and tumble sport. Injuries happened. But what Bonescraper's jockey had done that day was beyond shameful, even criminal.

As the story went, the smaller Nocturne appeared to have enough left in the tank at the last starting post to win. But as the race progressed, Bonescraper seemed to dominate, that is, until Nocturne made her move.

Flying full out, she'd moved to pass between Bonescraper and the cliff face in the final mountain pass before the drive to the finish. It was at this point in the race the incident resulting in Nocturne's injury occurred. After the race, Bonescraper's jockey claimed his dragon had the flight lane. He declared that Nocturne's rider urged his mount into a space too narrow for safe flight, which caused the collision between the two dragons.

Nocturne's jockey insisted he'd had plenty of room and that Bonescraper's rider intentionally directed his dragon to collide with the diminutive Nocturne, forcing her into the rock face. The race stewards ruled that the official camera angles in the mountain pass failed to corroborate either story. Thus, they had no choice but to declare Bonescraper the winner, as he had been the one to cross the finish line in front.

"As you can see, Nocturne's wound has healed," Cullum said, bringing Jackson out of his reverie. "But the deep scarring affecting the tendon's elasticity will be hard to overcome."

"Why doesn't she get up, Da?"

"I'm afraid that she's given up. She won't communicate with me. I know she hears me because she'll occasionally show a small response, but that doesn't happen often."

"Will she race again?" Jackson felt so helpless. Seeing such a splendid dragon brought so low caused a heaviness in his chest.

"Not unless she gets on her feet. She hasn't tried in two days." Cullum pointed to the small pile of waste near her tail. "The injury took more from her than her ability to fly. I'm afraid Nocturne may have lost her will to live."

"What are we going to do?" Jackson whispered.

"Funny you would use *we*." Cullum looked down at his son and then indicated the despondent dragon. "Here's my challenge to you. Help Nocturne re-find her fighting spirit."

"Me?" Jackson was staggered. "But I can't communicate with her. How am I supposed to help her if you can't? She trusts you. I've never even cleaned her stall."

"Jackson." Cullum never used Jackson's full name unless he was mad at him. "This is important. I want you to try. You have managed to bond with that little dragonet who has experienced nothing but abuse his entire life. How he would trust anyone is beyond me. But he trusts you." Cullum put his arm around Jackson and turned back to look at Nocturne. "Try to work the same magic on Nocturne. She needs you as much as Tivet does."

"But what if she attacks me?"

"She won't." Cullum squatted down to look Jackson in the eye. "Do this. Not for me. Do it for Nocturne. I know what you've been trying to hide, Jack. And you may have fooled everyone else, but you haven't fooled me."

Jackson's heart skipped a beat. *Does he know I can talk to Tivet?*

A wry smile twisted Cullum's lip. "You have the best eye for spotting talent I've ever seen. You know Luna is the better flyer, and you've recognized that she'll probably beat Nightwing by a mile, haven't you?"

"Yes." Jackson nodded, relieved that his secret was safe, though he didn't like keeping this from his father.

Cullum looked over his shoulder at the striking dragon lying in her waste and cleared his throat. "Helping Nocturne is beyond my power. I've tried. You might be her last chance, Jack. There's something special about you. And that special power lives right here." Cullum tapped Jackson's chest and pulled him in for a hug.

Jackson leaned into his da's hug, trying desperately to hold back his tears.

"From this moment on, Nocturne and Tivet are your only responsibilities. Your brothers and I will take up the slack with your other chores." Cullum straightened and turned to go, pausing at the stall entrance. "Don't expect a miracle the first time you touch her. If you can get her to eat, that will be an amazing achievement on its own." He cracked a wicked grin. "At least for now."

CHAPTER SIXTEEN

RELAXING AGAINST THE STALL DOOR, Jackson crossed his arms over his chest as he observed Nocturne. While she seemed content to ignore him, he knew better. She was most definitely aware of his presence. Dragons didn't need to look at you to sense your every move and breath. And though Nocturne wasn't raised in the wild, she remained an apex predator who relied on her senses, and that would never change.

Heaving a sigh, Jackson left the gate open as he retrieved the tools he would need to clean her stall. After all, it wasn't like she would get up and try to escape. If she did, his da would think Jackson had performed a miracle.

When he returned, as expected, Nocturne hadn't moved. Humming his mum's favorite Irish lullaby, he moved around the stall. His usual practice was to hurry and clean a stall while its inhabitant was out exercising. This time, he puttered around as he sifted through the bedding, fluffing as he went while avoiding the soiled area around Nocturne's tail, saving the most intrusive part for last.

"So, Nocturne, I know you don't want to move, and though you don't understand me, I'm going to need to get a little personal here." To keep from startling her, Jackson moved to squat down near her shoulder where her graceful neck curled around, her head resting on her foreleg, putting them on eye level. "Are we going to be okay with each other? Because if you bite me or flame me, I might not be able to get over that?"

As he blathered on, Nocturne's nostrils flared. Though it wasn't much, a slight sense of satisfaction sparked within Jackson. Anything was better than the unresponsive stupor the dragon had displayed to this point. Still, dragons didn't tend to behave well around the creature deaf. As a member of this underrepresented group, Jackson had spent a good deal of thought as to why that was.

He'd always wondered if it had something to do with the humans that they couldn't communicate with were considered prey. But he'd been around racing dragons long enough to understand they were volatile by design. Even the best-natured dragon could do the unexpected, leaving the possibility of someone getting hurt. It never paid to get distracted when working with a dragon.

Jackson tried not to tense up as Nocturne's eyes widened slightly, and she began to really look at him.

"You deciding how you'll deal with my creature deaf self?" Jackson fingered the bedding around her front leg, careful not to touch her. Building a little pile, he fluffed it and then re-spread it. Repeating the process several times, he tried to act like he wasn't alarmed by her inspection.

"Soooo . . ." Jackson drew the word out, puffing his breath toward her nostrils. "What do you say? Are we going to be friends, Nocturne?"

Nocturne blinked and fully opened her eyes as she drew in his scent. Her nostrils flared, exposing the red membranous lining. Then, with an explosive expulsion, she released all the air she'd drawn in. From the top of Jackson's head to where his knees rested in the bedding, Nocturne had sprayed him with warm, slimy dragon snot.

"Alright . . ." Jackson swiped a hand over his face. "I'll take that as a no." But she hadn't flamed him, and that was a good start.

He finished cleaning the stall, scrubbed the water trough, and removed the previous night's spoiled feed. Glancing back at the languid dragon, he wondered what he could do to get her to eat. Continuing to leave feed on the unlikely chance she'd suddenly reverse course and chow down hadn't worked. Lips pursed in thought, Jackson headed for the feed room.

"What's up with that?" Walking past, Brandon paused to close the gate. "You know better than to leave gates open."

"Leave it." Jackson stopped. "She's not going to escape. She won't even get up to eat."

"Nevertheless." Brandon started rolling the door closed. "Best practices keep all of us safe."

"Stop," Jackson raised his voice. "I told you to leave it."

Brandon's black eyebrows climbed toward his hairline.

"Look, Da told me Nocturne is my responsibility and that I could do what I wanted with her . . . within reason." Jackson cocked his head as he shrugged his shoulders. "He said whatever gets Nocturne back on her feet is okay with him. So, for now, the only thing I can think of is to try to gain her trust. And by leaving the gate open, I'm showing her I trust her. And building trust is a process."

Brandon took a moment to study his brother before glancing over his shoulder at the unresponsive dragon.

"Works for me. And it's about time Da trusted you with something more than cleaning up scat." His brother closed the distance between them and tousled Jackson's messy curls. Grimacing, he pulled his hand away. "Yuck, what is this? Dragon snot?" Not waiting for a reply, he reached over and scrubbed the slime off on the back of Jackson's shirt.

"Hey, knock it off." Jackson swatted at his brother.

Brandon just laughed and took a closer look.

"Nocturne got you good, didn't she?"

"She did," Jackson admitted. "It's a good sight better than getting flamed."

"Well, a good snot bath is more of a reaction than the rest of us have gotten out of her." Brandon studied Nocturne, who kept her eye on Jackson. "Little brother, if you can find a way to pull Nocturne out of her malaise, you'll have accomplished something truly remarkable." He turned back to Jackson, his tone somber. "I don't know how long we can keep the wolves at bay without her. We desperately need a win."

Jackson knew things were tight, but he hadn't realized it was as bad as Brandon's words implied. It was no secret that after Duffy Nolan had bought off all of old man O'Donnell's holdings, things had steadily worsened for the remaining racing families. Using Bonescraper and his sire Abraxas as a draw, Nolan was slowly but surely enticing the dragon owners in the area to move their stock to his racing stable. It seemed to Jackson everybody wanted to be on the side of the winning hand far more than they wanted to stay faithful to old ties. Yet, who could blame them?

The only client Jackson's family had left was Regan Malony. He'd been with them for years and always kept at least five dragons in training. Still, day training on five dragons barely paid the bills for a holding as extensive as the McLoughlin's. Ever-increasing land taxes alone were enough to eat a hole in the farm's annual earnings. And without purse money flowing in, day rates alone were not enough to sustain the farm.

"What about Luna and Nightwing? One of them should win that maiden race next month."

"They should. They both have enough talent. And barring injury, they've got the attitude to be good racers." Brandon ran his hand across his jaw. Jackson could hear the scrape of whiskers. "But . . ."

"But?"

"Word's been going around that Nolan has a good one of his own, and he's been getting it ready to debut in the same maiden race. It might not be as easy a win as we had hoped. Besides, even if one of them managed to win the race, the trainer's share of the purse money from a maiden race would barely pay the feed bill for one month. We need the type of payday Nocturne used to pull in. It'll be a few years before Luna or Nightwing has the experience they'll need to compete in graded stakes races." Brandon smiled. "But it sure couldn't hurt to put up a win. Even if it's only a maiden race."

"What about Regan's claimers? Any of them ready to race?"

"Rahu pulled a wing joint in his last loss. It'll be a while before he's back in training. Scyllar is rearing to go. But somebody will claim her right out from under us if we fly her where she belongs. Regan loves that dragon and doesn't want to lose her. You know how it goes when clients name a dragon after someone they love. It becomes personal. I don't know why people do that." Brandon scratched behind his ear. "He'll force us to race Scyllar over her head, which makes her unlikely to win. Regan's other two maidens are still a couple of months away, and we just got that baby in to break. It'll be at least another year, maybe two, before he's ready for a race."

Jackson knew all about the claiming races. Explaining to a client why their dragon wouldn't be the next Nocturne or Bonescraper was the bane of every dragon trainer's existence. Dragons needed to be flown where they could win.

In Jackson's opinion, recognizing where his charges belonged was one of a trainer's most important jobs. Getting a racer's wings jerked off in a race they had no chance of winning would only crush their confidence and ruin them in the long run.

Jackson may not have been allowed to help directly with training, but that didn't mean he wasn't paying attention. He'd figured out early on that instilling confidence in a flyer was crucial. Confidence, something Jackson found he sorely lacked. Despite his self-perceived failings, or perhaps because of them, he understood the value of keeping each dragon thinking they were hot stuff.

After cleaning the feed tub, Jackson placed it back in Nocturne's stall, intentionally leaving it empty. It wasn't about how wasteful it was to fill a feed tub only to have it spoil. It was an idea he'd been toying with while cleaning her stall, and he wanted to give it a try. If he denied her a full tub, something she'd only turn her nose up at anyway, maybe she'd appreciate her feed more the next time he brought it. He wasn't going to starve her. She was already doing a darn good job of that on her own. No, Jackson would set Nocturne's feed at the regular time, wait fifteen minutes and if she failed to show an interest, take it away. In the meantime, he needed to find something Nocturne would think of as a treat and would resent if taken away. But how would he get her to acknowledge something as a treat if she wouldn't even try it?

I can't exactly rub it on her lips as I did with Tivet. His eyes widened. *Or can I?*

CHAPTER SEVENTEEN

WHEN JACKSON RETURNED TO TIVET'S stall, he found the dragonet lying on his back, wings spread, and he had his legs stuck straight up in the air. While his new friend may have looked ridiculous, the sight filled Jackson with anxiety.

"Hey." Jackson fell to his knees beside the little dragonet. He touched Tivet's exposed tummy. "You sick?"

~No, why would you think that?

"I've never seen a dragon lying on his back with his legs flapping in the wind. Unless they were sick . . . maybe not even then. You scared me. I thought you were colicky. Remember, Da said it could happen."

~I didn't mean to scare you. It's just that I've never felt comfortable enough to expose my underbelly before. This was . . . I don't know, liberating?

"Oh, I guess that's a good thing then." Jackson sat back on his heels. "But you know you don't need to be afraid anymore. We won't let anything happen to you. I promise. You're safe here."

Tivet locked gazes with Jackson for a moment. Then he rolled to his feet. *~You shouldn't make a promise you can't keep.*

"Why ever not?" Shocked, Jackson also rose to his feet. "You're my responsibility, and I won't let anyone hurt you."

~*You might want to, but you're just a scrawny kid like me. We have no power. We're only two potential victims of anyone bigger and stronger than us.*

Jackson considered Tivet's words. *Did being born creature deaf make me a target? Or is it my lack of confidence that's turned me into one?*

"If I've been a victim, then I don't want to be one any longer. And you shouldn't either. I say let's change ourselves."

~*And just how are we going to do that? We can't change what we are.*

"Not what. Who. We can work at making ourselves physically stronger, and we need to be smarter about . . . well about everything. Tivet, we have a choice. We don't have to accept this. I'm willing to try, are you?"

~*What do you have in mind?*

"One step at a time. Step one, let's stop feeling sorry for ourselves."

~*That might be more difficult than you think.*

"The way I see it, that will be the easy part. We have each other. We're a team. Together, we can do this."

~*This?*

"This starts with you getting healthy. From now on, you'll be eating properly; that alone is a huge first step. Secondly, how about a good scrub? You'll feel better after we rinse away the last vestiges of that Travellers' camp from your scales." Looking for agreement, Jackson ran the tips of his fingers over the rough scales on Tivet's long neck. "Don't you think?"

~*Bath? Like with soap and water?*

"Yep, and if we go to the pond, we'll be able to get you really clean."

~*Now?*

"No, it's too late to do it today. Tomorrow, once the sun is up, it'll be nice and warm."

~*I don't know how to swim, and I'm afraid of the water.*"

"You don't have to know how to swim. You're only going in the water long enough to get your wings wet, and then I'll give you a good soaping. We'll use the pond to rinse off the sludge." Jackson fingered Tivet's wing. "It might take more than one go."

~*Sludge?*

"Trust me, you'll feel like a new dragon."

CHAPTER EIGHTEEN

IT WAS EARLY MORNING AND JACKSON'S favorite time of day. He liked the crack of dawn. That brief period before the rest of the world awoke. A cacophony of sounds slowly filling the air, heralding life's renewal.

Despite this appreciation, Jackson was inclined to wake up grumpy and taciturn. But not this morning. Dew still clung to the grass, and the sun warmed the air, reflecting silver and gold over the pond's surface.

Carrying a bucket filled with the tools he'd need to scrub the dragonet clean, Jackson's step was light, and he felt—maybe for the first time—excited about the future. He glanced back at the reason for this feeling and couldn't suppress the laugh that bubbled to the surface. What a sight the melodramatic dragonet made—a gloomy Tivet whose head barely cleared the ground. With wings unfurled, Tivet dragged himself along, leaving a distinctive trail in the dew-heavy grass.

"Oh, come *on*. Do you have any idea how ridiculous you look?"

~*I don't care.*

"You should care." Jackson stopped, waiting for Tivet to catch up. "I haven't said anything about it before, but you stink."

~I don't care. Besides, you stink too.

"No, I don't. My mum makes me take a bath every day."

~Exactly. The stink of the perfume you use burns my nostrils.

"That's soap. You'll get used to it. Way better than rancid body odor."

~To each his own.

"Stop putting this off. Just grow up. You're getting a bath already."

~So, you're going to force me to do something I don't want to do. How does that make you any different than the Travellers?

Stunned by Tivet's words, it took a moment before Jackson could bring himself to respond.

"You know, Tivet, that you would even say that to me . . . well, it's hurtful. I won't force you to do anything. If that's what you think, I'll head back to the barn and get on with the chores I should be doing instead of helping you. Roll over in the grass like a spoiled brat, stick your feet in the air, see if I care." He stomped past Tivet, headed for the barn. All the excitement he'd been feeling was gone.

He was halfway to the barn when he heard a splash. Turning back, he found Tivet up to his knees in the pond. Concentric circles radiated across the water's surface.

~Please don't hate me. I'll be good, I promise. Please don't take me back. His unusual blue eyes were now the color of arctic ice.

Jackson's heart seized in his chest. This helpless, abused dragonet was far more broken than Jackson had ever considered himself. He may have been born with a handicap but it was into a loving family. Tivet was hatched into a cruel world surrounded by people who abused and hated him. No comparison could be made between their separate experiences. Jackson couldn't have felt worse.

"You'll never go back, Tivet. Never. As long as I'm breathing, you will not suffer at the hands of those people again. I will die before I let that happen." Setting the bucket on the shore, he waded into the water. "You're my cully, my compeer."

Tivet snaked his long reptilian neck around to rest his head on Jackson's shoulder. In response, Jackson gently ran his hands over Tivet's roughened scales.

"What do you say? I'm sorry. You're sorry. Shall we put this behind us and remove the remnants of the Travellers' abuse from your body?"

Later, back on shore, as they enjoyed the warmth of the sun and the fresh smell of the plush grass, Jackson ran the rub rag over Tivet's face. His eyes no longer whirled with shifting colors, and he'd ceased trembling. A sound of contentment rumbled from within his chest.

"You sound like a rusty tractor." Jackson laughed and reached for a spray bottle. "So, you going to admit that getting a bath wasn't so bad?"

~You were right—well, except for the scrub brush around my bottom. That was . . . uncomfortable.

"Yeah, I wouldn't like that either." Jackson cringed. "But from now on, since we got all the crusty bits off, we'll be able to use a sea sponge for bathing."

~What's that? Tivet sniffed at the bottle Jackson held. Wrinkling his nose, he snorted, trying to clear his nostrils. ~That smells like poison.

"In a way, that's what it is. Though it's not poisonous to you or me, it smells like it to flies and gnats and repels them. Pesky little buggers. They'll drive you crazy, buzzing up your nose and into your eyes."

~I'm familiar. The Travellers' camp attracted them.

"Well, let's make sure they don't bother you here. I'll spray you all over, and when I get to your head, keep your eyes and nostrils closed until after I've wiped the spray off. It'll sting if you don't. Let's start with your belly."

CHAPTER NINETEEN

CULLUM FELT HIS HEART LIGHTEN as he watched his son interact with the tiny dragonet. Jackson practically glowed with joy. The same couldn't be said for Tivet, who obviously wasn't enjoying the experience. Head down, long wings limp, a complete picture of discontent. Still, he submitted to the indignities of being scrubbed free of a lifetime's worth of ground in grime without resistance.

Cullum waited until Jackson finished gathering his tools, putting them in a bucket before making his presence known. Jackson waved in acknowledgment as he climbed the gentle slope to the quarantine barn with Tivet dragging a few feet behind. Cullum had to try hard not to laugh at the woebegone creature.

"That seemed to go well," Cullum observed as the two stopped before him. "Where's Tivet's lead shank?"

"He doesn't need one."

"Dragons need to be kept under control at all times." A frown creased Cullum's brow. "Why do I need to tell you this? You know better."

"Tivet can't outrun me, and he can't fly, so why would I

need to put a halter and shank on him?" Jackson laid his hand on Tivet's shoulder. "I'm trying to get him to trust me."

"It's not about trust, Jack. It's about control. You're the boss, and he needs to understand that from the beginning. You're not doing him any favors by not clarifying your expectations."

"I'm not his boss. I'm his friend."

Cullum stared at his son. How was he going to respond to that? If Tivet were a border collie, Cullum wouldn't object to Jackson calling the dog his friend. Rubbing a hand over his jaw, he finally shook his head and raised both hands in surrender.

"All right. For now, I'll suspend that rule." Cullum extended a finger and pointed it at Jackson. "But only for Tivet. I better not see Nocturne following you around without a halter and lead shank, understood?"

"Yeah, I don't think that will be a problem."

"I noticed you'd cleaned her stall and the empty feed tub. Did you get her to eat?" Which was why Cullum had come to find Jackson in the first place.

"No, when she ignored her dinner last night, I cleaned the tub and put it back empty. Each time I feed her, I plan to give her fifteen minutes to show an interest. And if she doesn't, I'll take it away. She needs to understand that what she's given can just as easily be taken away. A full bowl going to waste is no longer an option. If she doesn't want to eat it, Tivet will."

It was a clever plan on Jackson's part and was something Cullum had tried himself on dragons who were off their feed. But with Nocturne, it was different. Dragons could go a long time without food. Still, there came a time when it became dire. And that time wasn't far off in Nocturne's case. He didn't want to have to use a tube to feed the proud dragon. While it remained a viable option, it would only be a last resort when all else had failed.

"It's worth a try, but not for long, Jack. She's been off her feed for too long. We might have to try something else." Cullum warned, eyeing the earnest young man before him. "You got any other ideas?"

"I was hoping you might know if she has any favorite treats?"

"Not that I'm aware of. Up until the injury, Nocturne had always been a very good doer. She cleaned up anything you put in front of her. This . . ." Cullum shook his head. "Is a recent development. I'm afraid it goes deeper than what's obvious on the surface."

"I've had another idea I might try. If it works, I'll tell you about it." Jackson suddenly recoiled, jerking his hand from where it rested on Tivet's shoulder.

"What. Is. That?" Jackson pointed at the dragonet.

Cullum leaned in to get a better look. What had been black scales were quickly disappearing under a moving carpet of white fluff.

"Lice. He's covered in Dragon Lice." Cullum's disgust was quickly consumed by outrage. How could anybody neglect an animal to this degree? With that load of lice sucking the life right out of the little scamp, it was a wonder Tivet wasn't already dead. "What did you bathe him in?"

"I used the anti-bacterial shampoo Doc left. Then I used fly repellent."

"Doc called. He has the results of the blood tests, and he wants to discuss them with us. He'll be here later this afternoon. We'll have him look at this while here." Cullum indicated the moving blanket of fluff with a wave of his hand. "Before I forget, did you get the fecal sample he requested?"

"Yes, but it wasn't much."

"He only needs a dab to check for worms." Cullum pointed at Tivet. "Put him back in the pond, rinse away this load of lice, then spray him with the fly repellent again. I suspect it's that and not the shampoo killing this scourge. Shower and change your clothes before you handle Nocturne. I don't want to see her invested with these bloodsuckers. Something like this could be the last straw for her. And don't forget to disinfect your Wellies." He pointed at the boots Jackson had tucked under his arm.

CHAPTER TWENTY

JACKSON WAS ROOTING AROUND IN the pantry when his mother cleared her throat.

"What are you looking for, Jack?"

"This." He pulled a can of tuna out of his pocket and set it back on the shelf where she could see it. "Do we have any more of these?"

"Tuna? You hate tuna."

"I had an idea and wanted to try it out." Jackson dipped his chin to peer through his eyebrows. He felt sheepish as the tips of his ears warmed. It wasn't like everyone in his family didn't know about his aversion to fish.

"You aren't thinking about feeding that to your dragonet, are you?" Lorelei stepped into the crowded pantry and moved the can back to its proper place.

"Because if you are, let me disabuse you of that idea before it takes root. Canned tuna is for humans, not dragons. This entire can wouldn't put a thin coat over his tongue."

"It's not for Tivet. He's eating fine. I want to see if it'll get Nocturne's attention. I doubt she's ever had fish. Da couldn't remember her having a liking for treats."

"No, I can't say she ever did. Your grandpa said she took to training with literally no persuasion." Lorelei's eyes became unfocused as she thought back. "She's always been so docile. And yet she possessed a steel core when it came to racing. I can still remember her eyes when she readied for a race. They blazed with determination, and you knew that when her wings unfurled, she'd seek the win and that nothing less would do." Lorelei took the can from the shelf and handed it to her son.

"If you think this will help Nocturne, then good luck to you." She pulled Jackson in for a hug. "I think you might be exactly what she needs to pull her out of this funk she's gotten herself into." Lorelei leaned back. "But don't for one minute think that it's your fault if she doesn't." Holding her son at arm's length, she tightened her grip on his shoulders. "I won't have it, you hear me? So far, not one of us has been able to make a difference, and that's despite years of hard-gained knowledge at training all kinds of dragons." Her smile always made Jackson feel better. "I know this is a lot of responsibility." Lorelei lightly tweaked his ear. "But you're up to it."

"I am, and I won't let you down." Jackson ducked back in to hug his mum. "And I won't let Nocturne down either."

"How did I ever get so lucky?" Lorelei sighed, resting her chin on his copper curls.

"Lucky?" Jackson pulled away.

"That I would be blessed with a son like you." Before Lorelei turned away, she stroked his cheek lovingly. "Even if you do kick your dirty underwear under the bed."

"I never . . ." Jackson sputtered, embarrassed.

"Right. Must've been the wee folk then." His mum's laughter faded as she walked away.

CHAPTER TWENTY-ONE

JACKSON DROPPED THE TUNA OFF in the feed room before heading to the quarantine barn, where he found his da and Doc Miller looking over a document. Tivet lay curled on his bedding, feigning sleep. But he didn't fool Jackson.

"Strange? What do you mean by strange?" Cullum peered at the printout as he questioned Doc. "Like a strange disease?"

"No. He's not sick." Doc pointed toward the bottom of the page. "All of his counts are fairly normal, though on the low side of the range. It's understandable, considering his physical condition. But here," Doc tapped the page, "this count is bizarre. I've never seen anything like it. The red blood count is way too high, even for a healthy racing dragon. Let alone one infested with dragon lice, and who knows how long that's been the case. I would expect him to be anemic, along with a high white cell count."

"So, what's the takeaway?" Cullum glanced at the pathetic creature at his feet. "Considering how bad he looks, what's your prognosis?"

"It means his hemoglobin's elevated when it shouldn't be, which is exactly my point. Unless his heart is failing. And I don't think that's the case. It sounds normal, though we could do an EKG. But in my opinion, that would be a waste of money, particularly since there are no other indicators for heart failure. If you were to take in the strange blood count and his unusual anatomy, I'd be inclined to think he was born this way . . ." Doc shifted uncomfortably. "Like, oh, I don't know, that perhaps he's a different species of dragon entirely."

"What?" Cullum looked flabbergasted. "You think that this is some mutated subspecies?" He waved his hand at the dragonet. "I would hardly think that's a possibility. He might be different, but he's unquestionably a dragon. Though not a very handsome one, to be sure."

"I'm saying it would be prudent to wait for the DNA results before we jump to any conclusions. And as for a prognosis, I can't give you one." He pointed at the document. "This is beyond my experience. Let's wait and see."

"Wait and see?" Cullum lifted his cap and knuckled the top of his head. "Your words would suggest that this creature belongs to an entirely different dragon species. Yet we both know that's impossible. They're all extinct."

"I don't know what to tell you, Cullum." Doc pointed to the printout again. "The results don't lie. And I've failed so far to come up with another explanation. Believe you me, I've tried."

~*What are they talking about? Are they going to kill me?* Tivet raised his head.

~*No. Never.* Jackson entered the stall and stood next to his da. "What's going on?"

"Well, it seems you've managed to find yourself a very unusual dragon." Cullum put his arm around Jackson's shoulders. "How unusual? We don't know yet. But rest assured, we'll figure it out."

"Is he going to be all right?" Jackson's voice trembled. He wasn't sure his legs would hold him.

"All right? Jack, this dragon will be a lot more than all

right," Doc said. "If there aren't any underlying conditions causing this high RBC." Doc nodded at the printout. "Once he's in tip-top condition, a normal count for him could be mindboggling."

"And what would that mean?" Despite Doc's evident enthusiasm, Jackson's anxiety remained high.

"RBC relates to hemoglobin. Hemoglobin is responsible for, among other things, oxygenating the blood. With the possibility of a hemoglobin count like we're talking about, Tivet could fly longer, faster, and maybe even higher than any dragon we've ever seen." Doc waved his arms as he spoke, his excitement obvious. "Can you imagine the possibilities?"

"You mean he could be a racing dragon?" Jackson's voice filled with wonder.

"Whoa, let's take a step back here." Cullum pointed at Tivet. "Look at him, Jack. He's stunted, and that's something he may never overcome. I'm not aware of miniature dragon racing, are you? So don't be flirting with the idea that he'll ever be a racing dragon." Cullum squatted down to look into Tivet's swirling blue eyes. "It's not possible."

"He doesn't have to be." Jackson sat in the bedding next to Tivet, moving his head onto his lap. "But he's more special than you think."

"As are you." Cullum smiled as he watched his son defend his dragonet. "As are you."

CHAPTER TWENTY-TWO

HUMMING THE FAMILIAR LULLABY AND feeling a little more sure of himself—after all, he still hadn't been flamed—Jackson moved around Nocturne's stall, fluffing the straw. The muddied ground around the water trough indicated she'd been up at least once during the night to drink, but there was no sign she'd done anything more.

He went outside, put the pitchfork away, and retrieved her feed tub. Sure that she still wouldn't eat anything he gave her, he'd put Tivet's ration in the bottom of her much bigger tub and when she didn't eat it, he planned on transferring it to Tivet's bowl.

"Here you go, my beauty, eat up. It's a little different than what you're used to, but you'll like it. Tivet certainly does. You don't know Tivet, but you will." Jackson nattered along as he set the tub in its usual place, then picked up the jar of lanolin he'd left by the gate. "I think you'll like him, and I plan on introducing you. He'll be so impressed. But I can't do that until he's clear of dragon lice. Dragon lice are the worst, you know. You can't just kill the adults. You have to kill the nymphs, and that still leaves the eggs left to hatch—got to wait to get them too, or we'll have to start the process over again once that lot's matured and start to reproduce. It's a real hassle."

Keeping up the chatter, Jackson moved around to Nocturne's injured leg. Unscrewing the lid from the jar of lanolin, he ran his fingers through the waxy substance. Moving slowly, he carefully touched the inflamed flesh. When she didn't react, he smeared a gob of the emollient over her hock. Tacky at first, the egg-yolk-colored wax began to warm between his hand and Nocturne's scales. And as it did, Jackson worked it in, massaging up and down the entire length of the ugly disfigurement.

Humming quietly, he watched Nocturne, looking for any reaction to the food or what he was doing. With nothing forthcoming, he kneaded the scar for another twenty minutes before putting the lanolin away. Retrieving a rub rag, he used it to clean his hands, and starting on her tail, he ran the rag over her entire body. Inching along, he frowned at how the once beautiful scales had lost much of their sheen.

When he got to the base of her neck, where it joined her shoulder, he became more cautious, swiping the cloth over the graceful curve before continuing. Flushed with success, he gently rubbed both horns and each ear slit, determined he wouldn't stop. She needed to see that he wasn't afraid of her. Running the fabric across her broad forehead, he tenderly picked away bits of crust that had built up along the outer edges of her eyes.

Still humming, he paused long enough to retrieve a small vial from the pocket of his faded vest. The vile contained the oil he'd squeezed from the tuna tin. He grimaced when he realized some of it had leaked into his pocket. It didn't matter; the vest was a hand-me-down from one of his older brothers. Which one wasn't important, and Jackson didn't care anyway. Well used, the vest had long ago faded from blue to violet. Torn in places and covered in old stains, the garment resembled a dull mosaic. Still, it kept him warm; therefore, what it looked like carried no weight. He wasn't trying to impress anybody. What was the use? There was nobody to impress. Besides, what was another oily stain on the patchwork cloth?

But this dragon needed him, so Jackson wanted to make an impression. Carefully, he let a few more drops spill from the vial, further wetting the pocket lining.

Leaning over Nocturne's head, he took another swipe at her horns. As he reached further, he ensured the vest scraped across her muzzle.

It would have been hard to miss when Nocturne inhaled, and the cloth pulled tight against a giant nostril. Barely able to contain his glee, he stepped back and saw she'd cracked open an eye. *She sees me.*

"That's it for today." Jackson picked up the feed tub she'd ignored and left the stall, closing the gate behind him. When he looked through the metal bars, Nocturne was looking back for the first time.

His step light, Jackson fist-bumped empty air as he headed for the quarantine barn.

CHAPTER TWENTY-THREE

FEELING INORDINATELY PLEASED with himself, Jackson watched as Tivet gobbled down his ration.

"You know you're supposed to chew before you swallow."

~*That's not how it works with dragons. Our teeth are meant to tear, our jaws to crush. Chewing isn't a priority. Swallowing is.* He snuffled around in the dirt for anything he might have dropped.

"Well, that's charming."

~*Do you see a table here? Maybe when you invite me to eat with your family, I might be willing to nibble daintily at my food—maybe. No, not even then.*

"Yeah, I don't think that's going to happen. Mum doesn't even allow Spot to lie under the kitchen table when we're eating." Jackson hesitated before he added. "Speaking of Spot, if I introduce you to my dog, do you think you can refrain from hurting him?"

~*Dogs don't like me.*

"Spot will. He likes everybody. Da says he'd lick a burglar's hand before showing him where we keep the family silver. He said I should've named him 'Useless' instead of Spot."

~Why did you name him Spot? It's a terrible name.

"It's not a terrible name. He has a big black spot around his eye."

~Makes sense, I suppose. Why did you name me Tivet?

"I don't know. It just came out of my mouth. I didn't give it a lot of thought. It seemed right. Why? Don't you like it? You want to name yourself?"

~No. It's just that it seemed fitting to me, too. And . . . well, I can't help wondering why that is.

"Maybe it's just the product of two great minds, as the saying goes."

Tivet pushed the bowl around as he meticulously licked the bottom and sides, the tin rattling against the hard-packed soil.

"You're going to wear a hole in the bottom of that bowl."

~I'm still hungry.

"I'll talk to Da and see if increasing your ration is okay."

"Talk to Da about what?" Cullum appeared in the open doorway, startling both the dragonet and the boy. Tivet cowered in the bedding.

~You didn't hear him coming? Jackson mind-spoke.

~No, did you?

~Seriously, you can hear at least a hundred times better than I can.

~A hundred? You sure like to exaggerate. Tivet managed to throw attitude in his mind-speak.

"Have you forgotten how to answer a question, Jack?" Cullum moved into the stall and squatted in front of Tivet. Lifting the dragonet's snout in his palm, Cullum looked into the unusual eyes. "These eyes are so strange; I've never seen this color before, and the way they change . . . it's almost like they swirl." Cullum shook his head, then wedged his finger into the corner of Tivet's mouth. "Let's get a look at those mucous membranes, little one."

Tivet edged back. But Cullum had a good hold.

~It's okay. He isn't going to hurt you. He wants to see the color inside your mouth. It's a good indicator of health.

Jackson watched as his da pressed a thumb against Tivet's pink-tinted gum line, then observed the gray-colored thumbprint he'd created.

"That's good. Did you notice how quickly it pinked back up, Jack? And that means?" Cullum quizzed.

"Good blood flow. If it stayed gray, it would indicate we still had a problem. Anemia, fever, systemic shock. Colic." Jackson listed the most common conditions that pale gums could indicate.

"Very good, though as high as his red blood count is, you'd think his gums would be bright red. And if you looked closely and were to compare them with the other dragons we have, his still aren't as bright as they should be. Building him back up will take a while, and this won't happen overnight. So, what were you going to ask, Jack?"

"Can I increase Tivet's feed? He's trying to drill a hole through the bottom of the bowl, looking for more chow."

"Yes, but only by ten percent," Cullum said, still holding the dragonet's head. He smiled as he used his other hand to scratch around Tivet's tiny horn nubs. The dragonet closed his eyes in pleasure. "He really is endearing. I can see why you were so attracted to this little scamp."

With a final scratch, Cullum rose, crossing over to the bucket that held Jackson's tools. Retrieving a spray bottle labeled disinfectant, he sprayed his hands liberally before spritzing his boots, both top and bottom.

"By the way, Doc says that these dragon lice can be killed by almost anything. Pick your poison, disinfectant, fly spray, or insecticidal soap. So be sure to continue disinfecting yourself after handling him. Also, continue changing his bedding daily and spraying the area before adding more. And

I don't want you discarding the used bedding in the muck pile. Burn it on the bonfire. The adult lice don't last long once they're off the host, but there's no sense in taking any chances. It takes about five days of medicated baths to break the cycle.

"You've probably already killed off most, if not all, of the adults and nymphs. Once the eggs hatch, they'll become vulnerable to the insecticide, and with that, we'll have reached the end of their life cycle. It won't be long now."

"I can hardly wait. The thought of one more drop of blood being sucked out of his body gives me the heebie-jeebies."

"I'm with you on that. Your mum said dinner is about fifteen minutes away from being done."

"Okay, I'll finish up here."

Jackson listened to the sound of his da's footsteps fade away down the shedrow before he spoke.

"You starting to like my da?"

~I am, though he makes me nervous when he looks into my eyes like he's trying to invade my mind.

"He's probably still trying to communicate with you. I wonder why he can't. What's so different about you that it makes you unable to hear his commands?"

~You mean how I can understand yours while you can't hear other dragons? Is that the kind of difference you mean?

"Well, not just that. My brother told me they don't use words when communicating with the dragons." Jackson frowned. "He said it was more like they thought about what they wanted them to do, and they understood." He shrugged. "At least most of the time."

~They don't use words? Ever?

"Sure, they do, at times, but it's more like a word association. Like teaching a dog to sit or come." Jackson cringed at what he knew was coming after his careless remark.

~I am not a dog!

"That you are not." Jackson laughed.

CHAPTER TWENTY-FOUR

THE FOLLOWING DAY, WHEN JACKSON rolled back the gate to enter Nocturne's stall, she wasn't ignoring him. Her eyes were lustrous and alert, as though she'd been waiting for him to get there.

"Don't you look bright-eyed and bushy-tailed?" Jackson glanced at her serpentine tail. "Maybe not bushy." He strolled over and stuck the tub under her nose. "Got your breakfast? You interested?"

Ignoring the tub, she nudged it aside to root at Jackson's pocket. Laughing, Jackson set the tub in its place. As usual, he started to hum as he retrieved the pitchfork and muck basket.

Nocturne's attention remained focused as he went about his business. The stall looked pretty much the same as the day before. There was very little to show that the dragon had moved around more than on any other night. Working through the bedding, separating the soiled from the clean, there wasn't much to remove. As he neared her head, Nocturne again extended her neck to nudge his pocket.

"Oh, so you want some of this?" Jackson retrieved a sandwich bag filled with walnut-sized balls of tuna. He showed her the bag and removed an oily offering before putting the bag back in his pocket. Holding his hand outstretched and palm up, he waited for Nocturne to decide. "Please, please, please," Jackson whispered.

First, with her red-lined nostrils flaring, she sniffed before pushing the ball around with her snout. Jackson held his breath. Finally, she opened her mouth, and her fangs looked mighty big, hovering over his upturned hand. As delicate as a hummingbird drinking from a flower, Nocturne picked up the tuna ball and threw it to the back of her gullet with a flick of her head. Her eyes closed briefly before zeroing back on Jackson's pocket.

"Nope, that's all you get. Eat your breakfast, and then there'll be more from where that came from." As if she'd understood Jackson, she turned to look at the tub where he'd hung it, sniffed the air, then closed her eyes and settled back into the bedding.

It just couldn't have been that easy, could it? Disappointed, Jackson shrugged, retrieved the bucket with the grooming utensils, and began rubbing her down. By the time he'd finished working the wool wax into the surface of the terrible scar, in his estimation, time was up. He removed the feed tub.

Nocturne didn't so much as flare a nostril as he carried it away.

She can't live on fish alone. What if I mixed the tuna into the ration? I wonder if she'd eat it then?

Lost in thought, he nearly walked into his brother as Aiden led Luna from the stall next to Nocturne's.

"Hey, watch it, little brother." Aidan struggled to keep Luna from stampeding over the top of Jackson. "Mind your manners, Princess."

"Sorry, I was distracted." Jackson hurried to get out of the way. "Luna sure is on her tippy-toes today."

"That she is," Aiden agreed as he eased the beautiful dragon further into the shedrow. "She's peaking at the right time to be at her best for her maiden race."

"How about Nightwing?" Jackson glanced toward the stable yard to see if he could see the other half of the duo. The two always trained together.

"I'd say both of them are more than ready." Aiden peered inside the tub. "Is that all that's left of Nocturne's feed? Have you got her eating? Whoa, Da is going to be through the roof."

"No." Jackson's shoulders sagged. "She didn't eat anything other than a bite of tuna."

"Tuna? Are you feeding her tuna? Canned tuna? How many cans of tuna would it take to fill a dragon?" Aiden shook his head. "Yeah, I don't think that's going to be the answer, kiddo. You might want to try something else."

"Anything is better than nothing." Jackson felt hurt by his brother's dismissive attitude.

"Hey man, don't go getting all defensive." Aiden frowned at Luna as her chest started to glow. "I mean, it's not like you've had much experience with feeding the dragons."

"Maybe not, but I'm learning. So, unless you've got something positive to contribute, you might want to think about controlling Luna before she burns us both to a crisp." Smoke trailed from the dragon's nostrils as her tail whipped back and forth, the spikes gouging grooves in the shedrow.

"Easy there, Brown Terror." Aiden hurried to get Luna under control. As he led the prancing dragon away, he called over his shoulder. "Hey Jack, no offense, I was just trying to help."

Aiden's parting comment did little to ease Jackson's angst. It wasn't like he wouldn't accept all the advice he could get, but it did seem a little early on for his brother's critique.

CHAPTER TWENTY-FIVE

A WEEK HAD PASSED SINCE TIVET joined the family. He was out of quarantine, and Jackson was through the roof. Tivet ate three times as much as when he first arrived, and Jackson's da was impressed by his weight gain. But it was the growth in terms of height that was astounding. Where Tivet's shoulders had barely reached Jackson's knees, they now were level with his waist. Though the dragonet was taller, he wasn't getting rounder, as all the nutritious feed went toward the remarkable growth spurt he was undergoing. Dragonets grew fast, but this rate of growth was unheard of.

"If he grows any faster, he'll have to shed his scales like a snake. Nothing good can come from that." Cullum reached down to where the dragonet was lying in the long grass after his bath in the pond. Fingering a ragged patch, he pointed out. "See right here, the underlying hide is already cracking. Keep up the wool wax, but I think, in the future, you should start mixing in some royal jelly. Tivet's going to be vulnerable to infection until the fissures heal. The royal jelly will help protect him."

Jackson rubbed another dob into the area his da had

picked at. He peered under the crack. "He's black, so why does this look so pale, almost white under here?"

"Let me take another look." Cullum hunkered down and lifted the scale's ragged edge. "Hmmm, that is strange. But then, besides four legs, two wings, a tail, and horns, like any other dragon, there are many strange things about this little guy." Rising, Cullum wiped his hands off. "Keep doing what you're doing, son. Your dragonet is thriving, for now. How much he'll change?" Cullum shrugged. "Only time will tell. But I must admit I'm curious. Aren't you?"

"Oh yes," Jackson grinned up at his da in what had become a twice-daily ritual of bath, wax, and his da's inspection. "Can I take him to see Nocturne?"

"Nocturne?" Cullum's eyebrows drew together. "Jack, Nocturne could kill him."

"I don't think she will. He might help her."

"How would he help her?"

"I think she's lonely." Jackson screwed the lid back on the jar and rose to stand beside his da.

"Lonely? That's an interesting concept." Cullum smiled wryly. "You know that dragons tended to be loners when they were in the wild, right?"

"I do, but she's not in the wild, and her dam and sire weren't wild dragons either." Jackson shrugged. "Who's to say domesticated dragons haven't changed? Become more social?"

Cullum scratched at his chin, deep in thought. "All right, but I'm coming with you. I'll try to control her if she gets territorial or feels threatened." He turned and headed toward the training barn.

~You want to meet Nocturne, Tivet?

~You know I do.

~Even if there's a chance she might hurt you?

~I'm fast. She won't get the opportunity to hurt me.

Tivet was fast. There was no doubt about that. Jackson

had been playing with him every day. They ran and jumped, and Jackson was still quicker than the little dragonet, but not by much. Tivet had begun to spread his wings when they raced across the field instead of letting them drag in the grass. And as he'd steadily improved, he'd gotten more graceful. Tivet didn't waddle like other dragons when they weren't airborne. He was surprisingly fluid in his movements.

"You two coming?" Cullum called over his shoulder. "Let's get this over with."

"We're coming." While this was what Jackson wanted, he couldn't deny that the threat was real. He ran his hand over Tivet's head. Though still ragged and dull, the scales did feel softer due to the twice-daily waxing. Tivet leaned into Jackson's touch.

~Don't worry, I've got this.

~You've got this? Jackson laughed. ~Man, you're getting to be one cocky dragonet.

~If that's true, then it's your fault. I'm what you've made of me.

CHAPTER TWENTY-SIX

WITH HIS PRACTICED EYE FOR TROUBLE, Cullum glanced into each stall as he passed—a lot could be learned from how a dragon lived within its space. Creatures of habit, dragons tended to be pretty consistent in their behavior, especially when they were within their enclosures.

Knowing each individual, their traits, and mannerisms was important to a trainer. Each species had obvious variations in its physical appearance. These physical differences made recognition easy, as easy as a dragon was a dragon, as a dog a dog, and a cat a cat. But it was the mannerisms that made the difference. By making himself mindful of the subtlety of these differences, Cullum was one step ahead. Any deviation from an individual's typical behavior indicated that Cullum needed to look for an issue. No matter how insignificant it may seem at first, problems didn't tend to go away on their own; they only got bigger until they became apparent to all. Anxiety, depression, lethargy, lameness, and, in general, all illnesses had one thing in common: they started small and were easily overlooked.

"Nip it in the bud." Cullum's da had always preached. *"Pay*

attention, Cullum. Don't expect everything to be easy or to go as planned. Dragons stay up nights to ruin our days. You got the eye. Now learn to use it."

Cullum came to a stop in front of Luna's stall. The brown dragon was magnificent and probably one of the best he'd seen in years. Everybody had their eye on the more spectacular-looking Nightwing. But physical looks weren't everything. Luna had *it*. What dragon trainers and breeders called the look of eagles. If she stayed sound, Luna would outfly Nightwing every time. Maybe even challenge Nocturne's records eventually. And what delighted Cullum was that his creature deaf son knew it, too. Jackson might be creature deaf, but he was gifted with *the sight*. A talent none of his other sons had been blessed with. Hearing Jackson's laughter and Tivet's chirps as they entered the shedrow, Cullum took one last look at Luna before moving on to the next enclosure.

The joy he'd got from looking at Luna turned to ash the moment his gaze landed on his proud champion, Nocturne. Jackson had helped her, but not enough. She might have begun to pay attention when you entered her stall, but she still didn't get up and greet you as had been her wont in the past. Her eyes, dull and half-lidded, no longer glowed with radiance. Sadly, Nocturne didn't care anymore. Cullum could feel it in his soul. This incredible dragon, one of a kind, no longer cared about life.

He rolled the gate open as Jackson stopped next to him. Tivet trailed a few paces behind.

Nocturne lifted her head slightly when Jackson showed himself. Cullum glanced at his son. Jackson smirked as he withdrew a zip-lock bag from his pocket. Cullum heard, rather than saw, Nocturne's sharp intake of air. He glanced back in time to see her nostrils flare.

"What is that?"

"Tuna." Jackson opened the bag and withdrew a smelly,

walnut-sized ball of beige goop. Tivet's head snaked out, eager for the treat. Nocturne growled.

"You've been feeding her tuna?" To say Cullum was surprised would have been an understatement.

"She likes it." Jackson smiled as Nocturne rose to her feet. Though careful to avoid putting weight on the injured leg, she stood tall, her growl gaining in volume.

"Well, you better give it to her before she decides to eat Tivet instead," Cullum said.

"I have a better idea." Jackson offered the ball of tuna to Tivet, then pointed at Nocturne. *~Could you give this to her?*

~What? No.

~Please, Tivet, do it for me. I'll give you two later. I promise.

~You better. This is torture.

"Whoa, hold up there. You're going to get this guy killed." Cullum moved to block the entrance. "Son, you're not reading the room."

"She won't hurt him, Da." He offered the tuna to Tivet again. "Trust me."

Cullum threw up his hands, a grim look on his face. "Your mum will kill me if Nocturne eats him instead."

Tivet took the tuna ball, shuffled through the opening, and then dropped the ball in the bedding at Nocturne's feet. Lying down, he rolled over and exposed his soft underbelly to the growling dragon.

Her long neck stretched out. Jackson could see by the look on his da's face that he was trying to connect with the dragon. But it was just as evident that she ignored him. Instead, she thoroughly sniffed the tiny dragonet before pushing the bedding aside to retrieve the treat carefully. And that's when the world shifted for father and son. Nocturne didn't swallow the treat; instead, she nuzzled the little dragonet until he opened his mouth. Then, with great care, she dropped the tuna into his maw. Tivet glanced at Jackson before he swallowed.

And if that hadn't been enough of a shock, what Nocturne did next left even Jackson gob-smacked. She settled herself into the straw and used her head to scoot Tivet until he was cocooned between her front legs. Curling her long neck around, she began to lick him. Jackson felt his heart clench in his chest.

"How did you know she would do that?" Cullum swiped the moisture away from his eyes before he looked down at his son.

"I didn't. I just knew she wouldn't hurt him. I always have his scent on me. Nocturne had to associate him with me after all this time." He pointed at the dragon, who was purring loudly. "But . . . I didn't think she'd do that."

"I can't believe my eyes." Cullum put his arm over Jackson's shoulder and squeezed him. "How could we have ever thought you wouldn't be able to handle yourself around the dragons?"

"Do you think she'll let him leave?" Jackson asked, his voice thick with emotion. He wasn't handling his father's confession very well—his validation.

"Maybe, but for now, let's let them be." Cullum left the gate open. "Let's have a chat about that tuna, shall we?"

Jackson gave Cullum a worried look.

"Hey, I'm not complaining, but I think there might be a better and cheaper alternative." He smiled. "Mackerel?"

"Mackerel? Ugh, it stinks so bad."

"Exactly."

CHAPTER TWENTY-SEVEN

FOLLOWING A HURRIED TRIP TO THE fish market, Jackson and his da returned to Nocturne's stall, each carrying a tub with a smaller amount for Tivet and the other with slightly more for Nocturne. While Jackson wasn't surprised to find Tivet up and nosing around, he was thrilled to find Nocturne standing and closely watching Tivet's every move.

~*You, okay?*

~*Yeah, she's cool. Is that dinner? I'm starved.*

~*Can you communicate with her?*

~*Sorta. I hear her, but I don't understand her.*

~*Wow, maybe it's like a foreign language, and it'll take time to learn.*

~*Whatever. Feed me.* Tivet tried standing on his hind legs. ~*Smells good. What's in there?*

"He certainly likes his vittles." Cullum followed Jackson into the stall and waited until he'd set the tub in front of Tivet.

"Here goes nothing." Cullum set the other tub close to Tivet's as Nocturne watched suspiciously.

"Hey, slow down. You don't have to eat like a hog," Jackson said aloud for his da's benefit.

~I'm starving. You don't know what it feels like.

~I've been hungry before. Jackson responded.

~Because you missed one meal? It's not the same.

~Does it hurt?

~A little, but food helps.

~Could it be that your bones have been cracking and popping because they're growing so fast?

~Makes sense. I guess.

~We're giving you more tonight, and Da said I could keep increasing it for now. I suspect he knows what you're going through. But we still have to be careful.

Nocturne sniffed her tub and then snuffled at what was left of Tivet's. For his part, he gulped down the last morsel, and as usual, he proceeded to lick the bottom and sides until the aluminum tub shone. Raising his head, he looked at Nocturne's bowl, butted her out of the way, and dove into her untouched ration.

"Hey." Jackson went to intervene.

"No, leave him." Cullum put a restraining hand on Jackson's shoulder. "Let's see what she does."

Nocturne watched for a few seconds, then lowered her head and nibbled at the feed. Gently, she nudged Tivet out of the way and took a large mouthful. Undeterred, Tivet pushed back, trying to snag bits of the meat from around the edges. When Nocturne lifted her head, all but the tiniest bits of her meal were left, and Tivet wasted no time licking away the dregs.

"Now that is what I would call a success, wouldn't you? It's only a fraction of what she should have, but it's a start." Cullum grabbed Jackson and swung him off his feet, laughing. "Do you know what this means? At the very least, you've saved her life. Whether you know it or not, you may have also saved our farm."

Cullum set his son on his feet before he leaned down to

look him in the eye. "You did this, Jack. Nobody else, just you! By thinking out of the box, look at what you've accomplished. Don't ever think that you're not good enough. You're so much more than *just* good enough. We may have missed it before, but we see it now."

Jackson's heart thumped harshly in his chest; he'd never felt this emotional. He didn't know what to say, so he hugged his da as hard as he could.

"What do you say? Can you get Nocturne to leave the stall and start moving around more? If she doesn't use that leg," Cullum indicated how Nocturne kept the weight off her injury as she licked Tivet from his tiny horns to the tip of his pointed tail, "she'll never be able to get off the ground again."

"I'll try." Jackson held out a tuna ball. "Tivet, come here."

~You don't need to bribe me.

~I know. But Da doesn't know that. You're the one who doesn't want him to know we're communicating.

~True. Tivet put on a good show as he perked up, nostrils flaring before scampering toward the treat in Jackson's hand.

~Geez, don't overdo it. He's not stupid, you know.

~He'll only see what he expects to see.

~You shouldn't underestimate my da. He's the smartest person I know.

~Then why hasn't he seen you for who you are before now?

~I don't know that he hasn't. Maybe the chip on my shoulder kept me from looking past my resentment and jealousy.

Tivet stopped before Jackson. His neck extended as he bounced eagerly on his front legs.

"Make him wait for it, Jack." Cullum fell right into training mode. "He only gets it when you're ready to give it to him. You don't want him taking your hand off or ripping out a pocket whenever he sees you."

~I would never hurt you. Tivet sat back on his haunches. Sounding wounded.

~ Don't take it personally. Da should've been a schoolmarm. He loves teaching. Jackson tossed the tuna in the air. Tivet caught it with ease.

"So, as you always say, Da, there's no time like the present. Let's see what happens." Jackson left the stall with his da and Tivet close behind. "Is she coming?"

"Not yet," Cullum answered. Let's keep going. She'll either come out on her own when she's ready, or we will have to think of something else. Besides, knowing she's eating again is a huge milestone, and I will be more than satisfied with that today."

"Do you think she's still in a lot of pain from that leg?"

"She must be, but neither Doc nor I have any way of knowing for sure. Since she hasn't used it, the tendon will have shortened. That's a given, and with the obvious build-up of scar tissue, it'll take some time for it to stretch out. If it doesn't, she won't be able to fly again without the proper propulsion from those hindquarters to get her off the ground." Cullum lifted his cap, ran his fingers through his hair, and tugged at it as he resettled it back in place. "Still, she'll produce some magnificent dragonets."

Jackson frowned. "I've been massaging it twice a day. Do you think it'll do any good if I put more effort into manipulating it? My main objective is to soften the hide with the sheep wax."

"It's worth a try, but be careful. She's never been a biter, but if she feels pain, she might decide to hurt you back."

~She's coming. Tivet said.

Jackson looked back. It wasn't pretty, but Nocturne was trying. *Right now, that's all we can ask for.* Jackson thought to himself.

~Exactly.

~Stop eavesdropping on my private thoughts.

~You need to stop thinking so loud.

"Da, she's coming." Jackson tapped Cullum's shoulder.

"Yes, she is. Pay her no mind. Let's let her think this is her idea."

"How far should we go? What about a lead?"

"Not far, this time. She's only putting the barest amount of weight on the toe of that foot. And we won't worry about a lead right now. It's not like she's going to run off." Cullum shot a look over his shoulder. "Let's head for the wash rack; it's not very far. We'll give her a warm-water bath and let her dry in the sun. We don't want to wear her out so much that she won't want to leave the stall again. Like I've said before, I'm not sure, at least in part, that some of the pain she exhibits isn't psychosomatic. She's going to have to re-find her courage. Sometimes that's harder than overcoming the original injury."

"Tivet and I will help her."

~We can do it.

Jackson laughed out loud.

Cullum clapped Jackson on the back.

"I have every confidence in you two."

CHAPTER TWENTY-EIGHT

HAVING FAILED TO KEEP UP, JACKSON had his hands bracketed around his mouth, shouting encouragement between his bouts of laughter. Leaning against the barn, Cullum couldn't remember the last time he'd laughed so hard. The scene before him was so comical that he wasn't sure there was a person alive who could have choreographed a funnier skit.

"What's so funny?" Lorelei rounded the barn just in time to see Nocturne snake her head out to boost Tivet with her pointed snout. "Oh, my goodness, is Nocturne trying to teach Tivet to fly?"

"Yeah, I suppose you could call it that." Cullum gulped as Tivet went head over tail and ended up splashing head-first into the pond.

"Oh no." Lorelei made to push past her husband. "We have to help him."

"No." Cullum grabbed her arm. "He's not hurt. Let them have their fun."

Tivet rose from the pond, snorting water. Nocturne came to a stop and ever so gently grasped his neck in her maw. Stepping back, she dragged him onto the shore as Jackson arrived on the scene.

His face red from laughing, he gasped for air and flapped his hands as he tried and failed to get the words out around his laughter.

Tivet pulled away from Nocturne and turned his back on his companions. Cullum's lips curled as he realized that the dragonet was pouting.

"I never." Lorelei leaned against her husband. "That has got to be the cutest thing I've ever seen."

"Aye, the three of them would melt a heart made of ice." Cullum put his arm around his wife. "Have I ever told you how smart you are?"

"Not nearly often enough." Leaning into Cullum, she tipped her head up, and a warm smile spread. "But what did I do this time?"

"That." Cullum pointed at the scene before them. "You wouldn't let me send the dragonet away."

"You wouldn't have sent him away." Lorelei poked her husband. "You're just a rough ole cob who owns a heart of gold wrapped in corn silk. Layers upon layers of golden goodness."

"Yeah? You may be hallucinating. Have you been hitting the summer mead again?" Cullum kissed the top of her head, noting a few new gray hairs.

"Could be. So, tell me, how is our Nocturne doing? She doesn't look to be favoring that leg anymore. Has she flown yet?"

"No." Cullum's good mood evaporated. "I haven't even seen her try."

"Hmmm. What do you think it's going to take to get her back in the air?"

"Confidence." Cullum frowned. "A whole boatload of confidence. Bonescraper did more than damage Nocturne's leg. He stripped her of her courage. Metaphorically speaking, she had the heart jerked right out of her. And I'm not sure there's a surefire cure for that kind of injury. But if anybody can get her back into the air . . ." Cullum pointed. "Those two can."

"With your help."

"I'm not sure they need my help. There's something special going on between Jackson and Tivet. If I didn't know better, I'd think they were talking to each other."

"Communicating, in words?" Lorelei gasped. "Surely that's not possible."

"No, it's not."

CHAPTER TWENTY-NINE

JACKSON, TIVET, AND NOCTURNE lazed contentedly on the pond's lush green grass. Basking in the sun had become part of their daily ritual. Jackson rubbed sheep wax around Tivet's ear holes with one hand and worked on Nocturne's tendon with the other. Humming to himself, he smiled as the larger dragon started a soft rumble that seemed to originate from deep in her chest. Tivet lifted his head.

"Da claims that sound is a dragon purr. He says you often hear it when a mother dragon cuddles her young. I'm pretty sure that means Nocturne has adopted you."

~And you.

"Do you think so?" Jackson paused, surprised.

~She hasn't flamed you.

"That's true." His hands stilled as he considered Tivet's words.

~Hey, don't stop rubbing. It itches like crazy around my ears.

"You don't have ears."

~I do too . . . just because mine don't stick out and flap in the wind, like yours do. You know you could run faster if you

pinned them under a hat.

"Ha-ha, you're just too funny." Jackson leaned in. "Okay, let's take a look at those ear holes. They shouldn't be that itchy."

Jackson scraped his fingernail over the smaller scales around Tivet's ear opening. The dragonet twisted his head and leaned in to rub harder.

"Hold still for a second." Jackson frowned.

~Ahhh, that feels so good. Don't stop.

"Hmmm, this is curious." Jackson picked at a spot, and a small black shard flaked off. "Tivet, you're peeling. Remember how Da said that might happen?"

~Really? Okay, then get back to peeling.

"I'm not sure that's such a good idea. I think they might need to fall off naturally. We wouldn't want to damage the new scales underneath."

~Won't be any rougher than if I scraped my head against that gnarly old tree by the wash rack.

"You are such a pain in my neck."

~What would you do without me?

Jackson stopped picking at the small scales. "I'd be lonely and still hate everything about myself. How about you?"

~I'd be dead.

Momentarily taken aback, Jackson decided he wouldn't respond to Tivet's dark remark. It was just too sad. And besides, he didn't want to dwell on what would have happened if he and his brother hadn't driven into town that day. The day the Travellers decided they no longer wanted to keep Tivet around.

"Hey, look at this." A quarter-inch patch of scales peeled away, and what was revealed answered at least one of the questions they'd had about Tivet. The spiderweb of white cracks all over his hide was where the damaged scales had been attached and was now peeling away.

~I can't exactly see behind my ears. Unless you've uncovered a second set of eyes, and if you have, I can't see out of them.

"It looks like white skin." Jackson sat back. "No, it's more than white; there's something . . . I don't know, it's strange. I better get Da."

~No, wait. What do you mean white? I'm black. I want to be black. I like being black. Put them back.

"Tivet, I can't put them back, and even if I could, they'd just fall off again. Besides, it doesn't matter what color you are, as long as you're healthy."

~It's just that I want to look like Nocturne. Like I belong.

"You belong. Look at me. I have red hair and green eyes, but my entire family has black hair and blue eyes. I still belong."

~You didn't use to think so.

"Well, I do now. I'm going to get Da. You want to come?"

~No, I'll stay here.

CHAPTER THIRTY

THE FOLLOWING DAY, THE ENTIRE McLoughlin clan and Doc Miller gathered around the entrance to Nocturne's stall.

Jackson grew anxious; everyone appeared to have been struck dumb simultaneously. The night before, his da had seemed more curious than concerned over the strange coloring that Tivet's peeling scales had revealed. But from the look on everyone's faces this morning, Jackson felt that what had happened over the last few hours wasn't just meaningful; it would prove life-changing.

Overnight, Tivet had undergone a metamorphosis. There was no other way to describe it. Like a chrysalis birthing a butterfly, he'd shed his hide and emerged as a whole new species, the likes of which no one present had seen before.

"Have you ever seen anything so beautiful?" Lorelei finally whispered.

"No, I can't say I have," Cullum answered. "Not the color and certainly not the shape of those scales. They almost look like feathers. Have you seen anything like that, Doc? Is it a disease?"

"Let me get a closer look?" Doc took a step into the stall.

Nocturne was standing over Tivet, and the look she turned on Doc, he shouldn't ignore. Anyone who'd been around dragons for any length of time, unless *they had a death wish or were terminally dumb,* should have already left the area at a dead run.

For their part, his three brothers had remained silent, content to keep staring at the absolute wonder before them. None of them seemed inclined to weigh in on the remarkable sight. But when Nocturne hissed, that got their attention in a hurry.

"Hold on, Doc. She's not listening to me and frankly hasn't for some time." Cullum looked over his family, stopping when he got to Jackson. Can you get her to let us examine Tivet? He may look amazing," Cullum's tone didn't sound like that was necessarily a good thing, "but he seems unresponsive. We need the Doc to make sure he's okay."

"I'll try." Jackson reached into his pocket and pulled a fish ball out of the plastic bag he always kept well stocked. As he approached the agitated dragon, he started humming, the fish ball nestled in his open palm. Nocturne's nostrils flared, but still, she growled.

~*Tivet, are you all right? Can you talk to me?*

~*I'm so tired.* Tivet's mind-speak sounded weak, and Jackson's anxiety level ratcheted up another couple of notches.

~*Nocturne needs to settle down. Can you send some good vibes her way?*

~*She loves me.*

~*She's loved you from the first day you met. But we need to help you, and I don't think she'll let us do that.*

~*I can't see, and I'm scared.*

~*And that's why Nocturne won't let us in. She smells your fear. If you can show her you trust me, maybe she'll let me get close enough to help.*

~I've always trusted you.

~I trust you, too, and love you even more than Nocturne does. Can you send some of those feelings her way?

Nocturne stopped growling and lowered her head to nuzzle the beautiful creature at her feet. Tivet practically glowed in the shafts of morning light coming through the window. It was as if the brilliant colors of the rainbow shimmered softly over his body and danced in harmony with the sun's morning light. The contrast between the intense blue-black of Nocturne's scales made the pearlescent nature of Tivet's seem more pronounced. The two together were the very essence of light versus dark.

Jackson offered Nocturne the tuna ball again. She gently removed it from Jackson's hand and dropped it in the bedding before Tivet. Carefully rubbing Nocturne between her eyes, Jackson pulled out another treat for her. Again, she set it before Tivet.

~Can you smell the tuna? Jackson got down on his knees and pushed the black husk Tivet had shed out of the way.

~Barely. Is it tuna? Tivet's nostrils flared.

~Yes, do you need help finding it?

~Maybe.

~You are such a liar. Jackson chuckled, and a slight sense of relief passed over him. Picking the tuna out of the bedding, he tapped it against Tivet's lips.

~Here you go. Nocturne relaxed further as Tivet, one after the other, took the treats from Jackson's fingers.

~Doc is here, and he's going to examine you. I don't want you to be afraid. Jackson beckoned to the two men poised at the stall's entrance.

~What has happened to me?

~You shed your scales.

~Am I hideous?

~Tivet, you are the most beautiful dragon I've ever seen.

You light up the whole stall. You're beyond magnificent.

~Light up? Then what you said is true. I am no longer like Nocturne.

~You look like a pearl from the deepest depths of the ocean.

~I've never seen a pearl. I'm not even sure I know what one is.

~They're round and white, but it's like they reflect all the colors of the rainbow, and they're priceless. Just like you.

CHAPTER THIRTY-ONE

CULLUM RUBBED THE BACK OF HIS neck, nervous, as he and Doc approached the trio huddled together in the bedding.

"You're first, Doc." Cullum rested his hands on his hips. "I'm praying it wasn't a mistake bringing Tivet out of quarantine before we knew more."

"While we can all agree on the obvious," Doc said quietly, squatting beside Tivet, "that is undeniably a novel color for a dragon. I would wager it's not contagious."

"Novel might be an understatement." Lorelei laughed from where she stood outside the stall.

"Perhaps. Still, as surprising as this is, the scales are astounding." Doc paused, scrubbing his hand over his jaw. "If they can even be called scales. They're lustrous and look as though the light emanates from within. They're truly iridescent." He ran a finger over Tivet's neck. "And the *texture* . . . it's beyond comprehension." He exchanged a look with Cullum. "They don't just look like feathers. They feel very similar."

"Feathers? That's impossible." Brandon's lips curled down as he pointed inside the stall. "That's no bird."

"Hey, I'm just as flabbergasted as anybody else." Doc raised his hands as he and Cullum rejoined the group in the shedrow. "And though my good sense tells me otherwise, it doesn't change what's in front of my eyes. I need to study one of these scales under a microscope before making an informed opinion about its structure."

"If you value life and limb, I wouldn't suggest yanking out a sample," Lorelei warned. "Nocturne is completely broody over that dragonet. She may not have produced the egg Tivet hatched from, but she may as well have. As far as she's concerned, that's her baby. Trust me when I say you don't want to come between a mama and her get."

"You're right, and perhaps she's tolerating Jackson because she considers him a part of her clan," Doc suggested.

"Are you sure he's safe in there?" Aiden looked to his da for the answer.

"Yes, he's just as safe with her as Tivet is. Though we may have another problem to consider." Cullum smiled wryly. "Nocturne may be back on her feet, but she isn't responding to anyone except Jackson, and we all know he's creature deaf."

"Maybe so, but I'd wager he communicates with those dragons." Lorelei turned to watch Jackson whisper to both dragons. "Don't kid yourselves. They may not know what he's saying, but those dragons understand the goodness that lives in his heart."

"Can I take that with me?" Doc pointed at the husk Cullum had dumped in the shedrow. "I'm fascinated by the similarities to how a snake sheds its skin. However, our dragons do shed scales, though not like this, not all at once. Plus, Jackson said Tivet couldn't find the treat in the bedding. Which would lead us to believe he can't see. And since he's already shed this husk, you'd think that would no longer be a problem. When snakes shed their skin, they are temporarily blind. Perhaps in Tivet's case, the clear scale that covers the eye may be the last to shed. His eyes do look milky. But they're such an odd color that it's hard to say for sure. I managed to take another blood sample while in there, and I'll check to see if there've been any changes since the last time we tested."

"I hope we get some answers, and I'm as befuddled as you." Cullum sighed. "I've never been a fan of mysteries, and certainly not one as confounding as this little critter has become. I hope he becomes a blessing, not a curse."

"I don't know about a blessing, though it wouldn't be far off the mark to consider fate has played a part in bringing these three together." Lorelei took her husband's hand in hers. "Do you remember how we met?"

"As I recall, you fell out of a tree, and I broke your fall with my head." Cullum laughed.

"I thought you were dead, and then you opened your eyes." Lorelei seemed lost in the recollection.

"When I opened my eyes, I was sure I had died and gone to heaven." Cullum squeezed her hand.

"Oh, brother." Brandon snorted as a round of good-hearted laughter broke out and relieved some of the tension.

"I think we can safely leave this trio alone. Tivet seems stable, and only time will tell if his sight will return." Doc Miller considered the husk he held. "I can't wait to look at this under a microscope."

"Let me know what you find," Cullum spoke to Doc's back as he hurried away.

"Goes without saying," Doc mumbled, then seemingly caught by a thought, he turned. "With all the excitement, I almost forgot to tell you, another dragon returned with a torn wing after a training flight. That makes three. Also, I think you might be interested in knowing that another three groups of Travellers have set up camp at Nolan's place."

"What?" Brandon asked.

"Nolan's let them take over the entire west field along the

frontage road. And the other group, the one Jackson had the run-in with, joined them yesterday. It's something to see. It looks like a fall harvest festival with all those colorful caravans."

"Since when do Travellers and Dragon Speakers mingle? I don't like it," Aiden said.

"Do you think they've had anything to do with this spate of injured dragons?" Cullum asked.

"A few of the other trainers are starting to feel that might be the case. Mind you, they don't have any proof—just a big dose of speculation. You know how they are. If there's a Traveller in the vicinity, they'll blame them for everything that goes wrong and ask questions later. I wouldn't be surprised if an association meeting is called. I'll let you know if I hear anything." With that, Doc left the barn and headed for his beige truck.

"You know the first call the association makes will be to us," Cullum muttered as he watched Doc load the blood samples and Tivet's husk in the standard vet pack installed in the vehicle's bed.

"I could set odds on that," Brandon piped in. "The only thing that group agrees on is who to complain to."

"Maybe so, but we're all in this together." Cullum glanced around. "We aren't the only ones who've suffered since Nolan bought the O'Donnell farm."

"True enough." Brandon headed for the feed room. "It's time we got these critters fed before they start burning the barn down."

"Jackson, you stay there. I'll take care of mixing Nocturne and Tivet's feed. I think he deserves a little extra today, don't you?" Tivet started to squirm at Cullum's words.

"Thanks, Da."

"Was it my imagination, or did Tivet react at the mention of food?" Lorelei murmured.

"He may have. As I said, I've been getting more suspicious, but I hate sounding like a fool."

"Fool?" Lorelei laughed. "You're a lot of things, boyo. But fool is not one of them."

"We'll see about that." Cullum gave her hand another squeeze as they turned away.

CHAPTER THIRTY-TWO

THE MORNING SUN WARMED JACKSON as he and his father left the parking lot at the base of the slight rise where the parish church overlooked the small village. Saint Glendalough's whitewashed exterior and slate roof reputedly dated back to the 12th century. And as the world changed around it, the simple beauty of the church never did.

Today, Jackson could have happily lingered to admire the azure-blue clarity of the sky with its scattering of fleecy clouds being pushed along on a gentle breeze. However, he and his da were here for the weekly market. They'd come armed with a list of items they were expected to bring back to the farm. Included were the fresh vegetables, cheese, and milk ordered by his mum. And his da had commented when he'd climbed behind the steering wheel that he also wanted to get something special for her. A surprise, Da called it. And when Jackson asked why, his da had laughed. *"There'll come a day when you won't have to ask that question; you'll know why."*

Jackson fingered the fiver in his pocket to buy fresh mackerel for his dragon treats. He grimaced at the thought of spending the rest of his day cutting and packaging the smelly fish into treat-size pieces, a chore he didn't relish.

"You'd think you're training sea lions, Jack." Aiden would tease him each time he found Jackson replenishing his supply. This was just one of many good-natured jibes Aiden never seemed to tire of.

Veering away from his da, Jackson wound through the tents and booths erected for market days. Long-standing vendors had their patches staked out, claimed by tradition, so he knew where he wanted to go.

His nostrils flared as he passed the Bohemian Woods stand. Once—before the advent of electricity—it had been simply the Candle Maker. But when lightbulbs sparked to life, the vendors adapted to be the local purveyors of scented candles and soaps. Their sweet floral scents filled the air, competing with bacon baps and all the other scents that went along with a busy village market.

When Jackson passed the leather worker's display, he admired the dragon riding harnesses. Of course, they were all too big for Tivet, but Jackson couldn't resist running his fingers over one saddle in particular. The saddlemaker had precisely wrought a series of three overlapping spirals into the leather.

Celtic Triskeles were one of the oldest distinctly Irish symbols. The ancient peoples believed everything happened in batches of three. Jackson was very familiar with its form and what it symbolized. After all, it was prominently displayed on his family's racing silks.

The power of three. Jackson thought as he traced his finger over the design.

"Lovely, isn't it."

Jackson startled. He hadn't heard anybody approaching. Beside him was a small girl who reached out to touch the same item he'd admired. She was so frail and tiny; she could've been taken for someone much younger. Though dressed like a

Traveller, that wasn't the first thing he focused on. It was the white hair, eyebrows, and eyelashes. With blue eyes so washed out, she looked like she might've been blind. And her paper-white skin, without a hint of pigment, completed the ice princess look. Jackson didn't find her homely. Far from it. To him, the girl shimmered. She was beautiful. He found he couldn't stop staring. The harness was wholly forgotten.

"You don't agree?" Soft-spoken, her voice was sweet, and he leaned closer to take in every word.

"What . . . I'm sorry, what did you say?"

"You don't think this leatherwork is exceptional?"

"Oh . . . I do." Jackson refocused on the harness.

"Have you ever seen a dragon?"

"Of course, I have. This part of Ireland is known for its dragon farms. Why? You haven't?" He looked closer at her clothing: a long flowing cotton skirt paired with a colorful full-sleeved blouse. She also wore a woven crown of Pink Fairy's Breath on her head.

"Aren't you a Traveller?" When she didn't respond immediately, Jackson looked around to see if others were nearby.

"Is that a problem for you?"

"Then how have you not seen a dragon?" Ignoring her question, Jackson pushed on. "Travellers hunt them, even though it's illegal. They hate them."

"My mother wasn't a Traveller. She died, and since I had nowhere else to go, the government sent me to live with my father. And I don't *hate* dragons. My mother taught me that it's wrong to hate anything. Even a spider has a purpose." She gave a dainty little shudder.

"So, you don't hate Dragon Speakers or dragons?"

"Why would I?"

Satisfied with her answer, he stuck his hand out. "My name is Jackson."

"I'm Sarah." Her hand was so tiny and fragile that he was afraid to grip it too tightly. "It's very nice to meet you, Jackson. Do you live around here?"

"I do." He pointed south of town. "I live with my family on our dragon training farm, McLoughlin Racing."

"Oh . . ." Sarah clapped her hands together. "You have a dragon?"

"We have lots of dragons. Some are for clients, and the rest belong to our family." Jackson smiled. "But I happen to have one of my own. Tivet. You would like him."

"Can I come and see him?"

"Never." A tall boy with a thunderous look strode up. His hands balled into fists. "We don't associate with his kind, Sarah."

Jackson instantly recognized the bully. He'd never forget him, nor the stick he'd been using to torture a helpless baby dragonet.

"Toby, what are you doing?" She touched the much bigger boy as he squared off with Jackson. Toby pushed his chest out, his hatred on full display.

"I'm warning you, Sarah, stay out of this." Toby bumped his chest into Jackson, knocking him against the display of leather goods. "This girly boy has a lesson he needs to learn."

"Really? And just who's going to teach me that lesson?" Jackson regained his footing and pushed back. "You and who else?"

"I don't need no help teaching you to respect your betters." The bigger boy shoved Jackson harder, forcing him back a step. "I could do it with one hand tied behind my back."

"I think you'd need both hands even to find your arse." Jackson stepped up and shoved the bigger boy back.

Toby's acne-scarred skin grew mottled. Spittle sprayed from his mouth as he lost self-control and tackled Jackson to the ground.

Punching and kicking, they rolled in the grass, knocking over the saddles that leaned against the saddlemaker's booth.

Sarah tried to intervene, only to fall hard when the two boys tumbled into her.

"What's going on here?" Two gruff voices roared simultaneously. Coming from different directions, they waded into the melee, each man grabbing a boy.

Spitting and kicking, both combatants continued landing punches as they were drug apart.

"Knock it off, Jack!" Cullum, his fist tangled in Jackson's collar, gave him a good shake to get his attention.

As his da gave him a second shake, Jackson relented and watched as the other man said nothing, a smirk on his face as he held Toby by the arm. It was the same man who had sold Tivet to Jackson. And he hadn't lost any of his height or breadth. If anything, he looked bigger and meaner than ever.

"Are you all right, honey?" Cullum reached over to help the little girl to her feet.

"Don't touch her, you piece of filth." Toby appeared ready to continue swinging and lunged against the man's hold.

"Settle down, you eejit." The big man gave Toby an open-handed smack to the head.

"I'm okay." With Cullum's help, Sarah regained her footing, though she appeared unsteady as she looked at the bloody scrapes on her palms.

"You sure? You don't look okay." Cullum helped brush bits of grass from the hem of her skirt.

"That's enough, McLoughlin." The other man stepped forward and roughly grabbed the girl by her shoulder. "We take care of our own."

"I'm sure you do, *Lash*," Cullum emphasized the man's name. Jackson was shocked that the two knew each other.

"So, this is your spawn?" Lash gave Jackson a narrowed-eyed look.

"Yes, this is my son." Cullum kept one eye on the raged-filled boy standing next to Lash. "And there's no doubt that's yours?"

"And proud of it," Lash responded without taking his eyes off Jackson. "I remember you, the one who conned me into selling a dragon for a fiver." It wasn't a question.

"I didn't con you into anything, and it was a lot more than a fiver." Jackson was furious. "Besides, you'd have to think something had value to be conned out of it."

"That's enough, Jack." Cullum positioned himself before his son. "You don't need to defend yourself against the likes of *him*."

"The likes of *me*?" Lash sneered. "That's rich coming from you."

"We'll not be hashing this out again, Lash." Cullum turned to go. "Besides, what's your interest in that dragon? I'm surprised you even hatched him."

"Well, that ain't none of your business, now is it?"

"It will be if you start interfering in mine. Jack paid what you asked, and a sight more than a dragon who was no more than a week away from death was worth."

"They were going to eat him," Jackson interrupted, his voice laced with outrage.

"Quiet," Cullum warned before he continued. "So, I'd say it was my son who was conned. I'm pretty sure the Garda would be very interested in hearing about an underage boy being taken advantage of by a known criminal."

"You scut." Toby lunged for Cullum while Jackson darted around his da and plowed into the bigger boy, fists flying.

"Stop it." Cullum waded in, breaking the two boys apart as Lash stood by laughing.

"Can't say your boy don't have a bit of scrap in him," Lash said, crossing his arms. "A sight more than his old man."

"Shut your gob." Jackson struggled to escape his da's hold.

"I'm telling you right now, Jack," Cullum growled at his son as he separated the two boys. "If you don't shut yours and keep it shut, you and I will be having a conversation you won't like when we get home."

"That's it? What? You gonna take his milk and biscuits away for a week?" Lash grinned, pulling his smirking son back to his side. "Come on, kids. I don't know about you, but the stink of dragon scat is burning the hairs out of my nostrils."

Sarah, who'd listened wide-eyed throughout the heated exchange, hesitated and glanced at Jackson. She looked like she wanted to say something.

"Come on, Sarah, before I give you a smack," Toby growled.

"You won't be . . ." Cullum elbowed Jackson before he could finish his sentence.

"I'm sorry," Sarah mouthed before she limped away.

"Da, she's hurt."

"I can see that, but there's nothing we can do." Cullum frowned. His gaze followed the father and son as they strutted away and disappeared into the small crowd that had gathered. The frail albino child reluctantly followed, keeping her head down.

"We have to help her."

"We can't change the world, Jack." Cullum pulled him away. "She's with her kin, and that's all the government will care about."

CHAPTER THIRTY-THREE

JACKSON LED NOCTURNE FROM HER stall, and they were halfway down the shedrow before he heard Tivet scuffling along behind them. It had been a week since his transformation, and all his senses were back. Yet Tivet, restless and on edge, remained apprehensive. He hadn't left Nocturne's stall and flinched at every noise.

Withdrawn and uncommunicative, Tivet didn't refuse to answer Jackson when he voiced his concerns, but he declined to offer substantive dialog about what was bothering him.

"I'm glad you decided to leave him behind, Nocturne. He's pouted long enough over something he can't control." Today was the first time Nocturne had been willing to separate herself from the dragonet, despite Jackson's urging. She nuzzled his hand. While he figured she was looking for a treat, he liked to think she'd understood him. He tickled her snout with the hand holding the lead shank. Nocturne didn't need the halter and lead. She wasn't going to fly off. Still, he put it on to appease his father if he happened along; it wouldn't bode well if he found them traipsing around without the proper gear.

Stepping from the barn's shadow into the early morning sun, a moving shadow darkened the ground. Luna and Nightwing, with Aiden and Brandon aboard, were gaining altitude as they winged toward the training grounds.

A snotty nose had caused both dragons to miss the first maiden race they'd been pointed at. Now healthy, they'd both been training for a race to be contested the following week.

"Don't you miss flying, big girl?" Jackson leaned against Nocturne's shoulder as he watched the sleek young dragons grow smaller in the sky. Nocturne, long neck extended, continued to follow their progress. She'd be able to see them long after they became nothing but a memory in the sky for Jackson. "Come on, let's go stretch your legs."

Tivet lingered well within the shadow of the barn. Shrugging, Jackson broke into a jog. He wanted Nocturne to extend her stride and warm her tendons before encouraging her to increase her pace. Though her gait was near normal, Jackson still held out hope that she'd fly again, while the rest of the family weren't so sure. But he was well aware that before she could take to the sky, she would need to trust that the scarred leg would hold under the powerful thrust required to lift her massive body from the ground.

In hopes that Tivet would follow, Jackson headed toward the far end of the west field, where there were a series of stone outcroppings. Undulating across the land, they formed small terraces in the topography. Each step-down varied, some only a couple of feet, others as much as five. Jackson hoped that Nocturne would realize, as she negotiated the terrain, first on the way down but mainly on the way back up, that her leg would not only hold but that it wouldn't hurt either. If this went well, eventually, they could take on the higher outcroppings where she could spread her wings and soar from the edge. There was no way Jackson could keep up, but he'd worry about that when the time came.

Reckoning that Nocturne had stretched sufficiently, Jackson unsnapped the lead shank and urged her into a jog. As the graceful dragon extended her stride over the level field, Jackson had to run full out to keep up.

His da wouldn't approve of Nocturne being off shank. But it was Jackson's job to get her back in the air, and to that end, he figured he'd have to bend a few rules.

Nocturne twisted her head and eyeballed the first terrace. She stutter-stepped before the edge. Falling back, Jackson held his breath. *Please don't fall.*

The uncertain dragon protected her hind leg on landing, but she didn't go down and didn't hesitate as she jogged toward the next terrace. Jackson stumbled and slowed down; he didn't want to take a header. He still nursed bruises after his tussle with Toby.

And that wayward thought was all it took, Jackson's toe caught on a shard of jagged rock buried in the grass. Down he went and tumbled over the edge. As he landed on his back, with the wind knocked out of him, a flash of light filled his vision. It was Tivet. Wings spread, he'd followed Jackson off the terrace, and just like that, the little dragonet was airborne. It didn't last long. Still, it was flight.

Jackson sat up, gasping for breath. Tivet had flown. Granted, he didn't know how to stick the landing, going head over heels, but Jackson thought his heart might explode with happiness.

"Hey, you flew." Jackson crawled over to where Tivet slowly righted himself. Throwing his arms around the glimmering dragonet, he hugged him as tight as he could. "You are the best dragon in the world."

~You really think so? In turn, Tivet wrapped his wings around Jackson.

"Yes! And don't you ever doubt yourself again."

From behind him, Nocturne snorted, ruffling Jackson's

hair. Untangling himself, he reached up and placed his hands on her muzzle. "Hey girl, did you see? Our boy took his first flight?" Jackson looked between the two dragons that had become such a massive part of his life. *They are my life.* Warmth filled his chest.

"Aren't we just the perfect triumvirate?" Jackson's brow creased. "You know, we should have a name. How about the Triskelions? The power of three. I represent mental because I have been so stupid for so long, and long past due that I woke up." He pointed at Tivet. "And you represent physical because you've suffered from never having known a kind hand."

~Until now. Tivet interrupted, easing his snout under Jackson's arm.

"True." Jackson rubbed his fingers over the soft, feathery scales on Tivet's head. And you, Nocturne, represent the spiritual. You have to reclaim what Bonescraper took from you."

~I like it. Tivet agreed.

"Yes, the power of three. Three parts to make the whole. Mental, physical, and spiritual. Together, we can face anything."

Nocturne kneeled; Jackson was familiar with how the dragons would kneel on command for their riders to mount. But this was Nocturne inviting him to climb onto her back. Everything he had been raised to believe told him he shouldn't, but Jackson knew, as sure as he would take his next breath, that accepting Nocturne's invitation was right. This was the first step to the commitment they needed for this broken champion to find her way back.

He climbed up her leg and swung onto her sleek back. He looked down. Tivet glowed like an emerald, with the grass's dark green reflecting off his scales.

"We have a lot of work to do if we're going to live up to our name. You guys ready?"

~I am.

With Tivet hot on her heels, Nocturne jogged toward the next terrace. When she leapt, Jackson caught his breath as the ground fell away.

"Yes!" He whooped, his voice filled with glee.

CHAPTER THIRTY-FOUR

RACE DAYS WERE THE CULMINATION of a lot of hard work, and as far as Jackson was concerned, they were always stressful but a lot of fun. He found this especially so when one of their racing dragons was to make its first flight against competition. You always had a good idea as to the amount of talent any particular trainee had, but until they were tested in an actual race . . . you couldn't be sure. They could out-fly everything in the morning and end up dead last in the afternoon. It was just part of dragon racing.

Luna and Nightwing were flying in a Maiden Allowance race written for dragons between five and ten years old who had never won a race. There were also maiden claiming races on today's program—where the dragons entered could be claimed away from their owners for the price specified in the conditions—but neither Luna nor Nightwing was destined to fly in a claiming race. They were both too good to take a chance of losing one or both to a claim.

The race they were flying in would be contested at a distance of fifty miles, and as such, it was basically a sprint race for dragons. Considering the need to slow for the turns, the overall average speed for these babies would be forty-five to fifty miles per hour, though they could fly much faster than that.

The course covered five miles in a straight line, with three sets of flight pylons used as gates. One set was placed at either end of the course and one midway between where the race would begin and end. If viewed from above, the track would look like a giant figure-eight. Each dragon and jockey duo would fly the route ten times. Significantly, they must trigger race cameras with each pass through the different flight gates.

Dragons who flew too high or wide and missed a gate would be disqualified. The course was intended to test each contestant's agility on a short course before longer and more complex races were attempted in the future.

Jackson let his gaze scan over the six dragons scattered around the saddling paddock. Five were led by their grooms and paraded before the grandstand, where people hooted and hollered for their favorite. All but one of the dragons wore their numbered saddlecloth and racing tack. That one notable exception was Luna.

Jackson had eyes only for the brown dragon in the fifth stall, and his heart climbed into his throat at what he saw. Luna was particularly ornery about accepting the racing harness. The equipment used for racing was specialized, unlike what they used in daily training. And though she was familiar with the racing gear, she wasn't having any part of it on this afternoon.

The most significant difference was the elasticized girth strap rather than the padded leather strap they used for training. Luna and Nightwing had been schooled several times at the farm using this equipment, guaranteeing their familiarity. But it didn't seem to have made a difference in Luna's case. She was on her hind legs for the third time, wings spread, and the saddling structure rattled with each blow of her barbed tail.

Cullum took the lead shank from the groom and led her from the stall. Joining the parading dragons around the walking ring, Luna, neck arched, was on her toes, prancing around with her wings quivering at her sides. The expression on Cullum's face told Jackson that his father was communicating with Luna, trying to calm her down. They were halfway around the walk ring for the second time before she appeared to settle.

Cullum didn't hesitate when they approached the stall entrance, walking Luna straight in. Within minutes, the paddock crew had the saddle attached to the neck harness and the elastic girth pulled tight. But other than an occasional tail twitch, Luna stood with her head down, focused on Cullum.

Bright racing silks added jewel-toned points of interest to the already heady site as the first jockeys began to arrive. Plus, the sleekly muscled dragons, white tents flying their colorful pennants, and the grandstand filled to the top with people in their race-day best always combined to make it exciting for Jackson.

The overflow crowd jostled against the saddling paddock fence as they tried to get a close-up view as their favorites paraded by. Getting elbowed didn't bother Jackson—just another part of what made the experience so much fun.

A tap on his shoulder alerted Jackson to Robby's return. Scooting over, he made space for his brother.

"Here you go, ten quid on Luna. I have no idea what you've been looking at, as Nightwing and Luna have trained together. I should have booked this bet myself. Twenty-five-to-one odds on Luna? You know as well as I do when the price is that high, Punters should take note. Still, I've seen dragons who appeared to have no chance at all of winning do just that and at astronomical prices."

"Twenty-five to one?" Jackson gasped, ignoring everything else Robby was nattering on about. If Luna won,

Jackson could buy the harness with the triskeles engraved into the leather. For now, it might be too big for Tivet. But not for long, if the way he grew was any gauge to go by.

"Don't be counting your chickens before they hatch, kiddo." Robby had seen the look on Jackson's face. "There's a reason Luna's got that big price on her. She can't outfly Nightwing even if he had one wing tied behind his back."

"He couldn't get off the ground with only one wing," Jackson snorted. "What odds did you get on Nightwing?"

"Five to one."

"Really? Shouldn't he be a shorter price than that? He was a standout in his qualifying race."

"It doesn't matter. Word's out that Nolan's entered a real speedster, another son of Abraxas. They say he's just like his half-brother, Bonescraper. Mean as a snake."

"Which one is he?" Jackson grabbed the program from his brother's hand and looked up the dragon in question. "Askook?"

"You don't need the program. All you have to do is open your eyes. Here he comes now."

Parading with the jockey aboard, the fiery-red dragon headed their way, and the sight of him took Jackson by surprise. How had he not noticed this dragon already? Askook dominated the landscape. He didn't look like he belonged in this race. He was so big and mature; how could he fall under the ten-year age cap outlined in the conditions? The red beast had the muscle and physical presence attributable to a dragon twice his age.

"Did anybody check his teeth?" Jackson murmured.

Robby laughed and clapped his brother on the back. "You want me to try and get your money back?"

"Ha ha, Robby." Money laid was money spent. It would only return to Jackson's pocket if Luna outflew this behemoth.

When the giant's glowing yellow gaze flicked past

Jackson, he saw something he didn't like. He didn't know how he knew, but he did. This dragon was dangerous.

Suddenly, Jackson wasn't worried about losing his money. It was the safety of the other dragons that made him feel sick to his stomach—especially for dainty Luna.

CHAPTER THIRTY-FIVE

WHEN THE DRAGONS APPROACHED THE starting line, Jackson's heart pounded so hard he could barely hear the announcer's voice over the loudspeaker.

"Hey, calm down, Jack. You're too young to have a coronary." Robby rested an arm over his shoulder.

"Aren't you worried, Robby?" Jackson pointed toward the behemoth that dominated the landscape. He couldn't take his eyes off Askook.

"It won't be the first time I've contributed to the bookies." Robby laughed.

"But what if he hurts one of the other dragons?"

"They're all wearing anti-flaming muzzles," Robby pointed out. "You don't need to worry."

"I was thinking more about getting knocked out of the sky than being flamed. He's monstrous."

"That's racing, Jack." Robby raised his eyebrows. "How would you feel right now if Luna was by far the biggest?"

"Yeah, I guess you're right." Even that admission didn't sit well with Jackson.

"Besides, if he wins today, we won't have to worry about

him in the next race," Robby added.

"Maybe Da should petition the racing commission again about implementing weight divisions." Jackson mused.

"Da could have entered Luna in a Drakaina-only race, but it was decided that since Nightwing has a calming influence on Luna's flightiness, it would be best to race them together. At least for their first start." Robby said.

"Yeah, I know." Jackson followed the activity at the starting line, where the Starter directed the dragon handlers to line up in order by position number.

With the first gate being a left-handed turn through the towers, the dragon in the number one post, with enough speed, would be at an advantage going into the turn. On the downside, if the dragon couldn't get there first, they could get squeezed out and possibly miss the gate entirely—Luna wore the number one towel.

Using a slip line through the bridle ring, Cullum led Luna up to the start line, where she promptly reared onto her haunches and roared a challenge. Two positions down, Askook responded. Whipping his head around, he knocked his handler over just as the starting horn blared.

"Robby, Luna got left." Jackson gasped, horrified. Four dragons had leaped into the sky, gaining altitude with each successive downbeat of their massive wings. Both Luna and Askook were left at the start. Cullum, who'd released the slip line at the sound of the horn, moved to intercept Askook as he lumbered toward the smaller dragon, roaring his return challenge.

Jackson cringed, digging his fingers into his brother's arm.

"They'll be all right." Robby's words lacked conviction. Cullum was one of the best Dragon Speakers in Ireland; everybody knew it, but an ill-mannered dragon, out of control? It would be a miracle if Cullum could influence an outcome that, at this point, looked unavoidable.

"Get her in the air," Cullum yelled.

Luna's jockey tapped her smartly with his crop, bootin' and scootin'. He urged her to do what she'd been trained to do—take flight. Jackson took a deep breath as the brown dragon leapt into the air. Up she flapped, her lighter body mass making it easier for her to gain altitude quickly.

Askook's jockey seemed to have little control over the brute as he exploded from the ground, his massive hindquarters rocketing him into the air as he pursued the female that had dared to challenge him. Askook's downdraft knocked Cullum off his feet. Uninjured, he jumped up and stormed toward the official's stand.

With Askook's bulkier body, it took him longer to gain altitude, and Luna quickly widened the gap between them. Jackson raised his binoculars, looking to the rest of the field where Nightwing was clearly in the lead. But they still had a good distance before reaching the two pylons that marked the first flight gate.

As the minutes ticked away, Luna began to close on the leading pack. Slowing as he maneuvered through the first flight gate, the black dragon maintained his advantage over the rest of the field.

"Jackson, look." Robby pointed toward the massive screens above the grandstand, displaying the action as it took place.

What Jackson saw made his blood run cold. Askook was quickly gaining on Luna. It was apparent to everyone watching that the red dragon still refused to take direction from his jockey. Out of control, Askook flew an intercept course with Luna.

As gate after gate was traversed, Jackson's chest filled with dread. There couldn't be a soul within the crowd that thought Askook's intent was anything other than to harm the young female once he caught up to her.

At one point, as the race was close to its end, Luna's jockey glanced over his shoulder, fully aware of the danger as he and his mount approached another flight gate. Clinging to Luna's harness, the rider directed her into a steep dive to gain speed, then urged her to bank hard through the gate.

"He's gonna scrape the paint," Robby whispered, uttering an old racing term from when the gates had once been painted wooden towers rather than the current air-filled silk. Harris, Luna's jockey, was Jackson's favorite rider. Experienced and talented, Harris took the time to come to the farm and familiarize himself with each of its dragons before he rode them on race day. As a result, Harris knew Luna and her abilities as well as anyone. Still, he was taking a humongous risk. If his mount came too close, and even though the silk pylon was designed to tear away, any number of tragic events could be set in motion at the speed and angle they approached. Not the least of which was Luna getting entangled and going down.

Jackson was so frightened that he wanted to close his eyes, but he was glad he hadn't when Harris's strategy paid off and Luna made a clean turn. Harris then urged her to use the momentum she had gained with the dive to propel herself, like the crack of a bullwhip, back to race elevation with minimal exertion. It was a brilliant move, and few would have had the nerve to attempt it.

Jackson whooped in delight when Askook took the turn without a speed reduction and clipped the pylon. He was forced to straighten out of the turn, losing speed and distance on the more maneuverable drakaina.

Relaxed and in control, Luna continued to gain on the field with each turn until she was heads-up with the trailing dragon. At this point, with one lap to go, Harris gave the talented Luna her head. She swooped past the competition, and once around the last turn, there was only one dragon to catch. Nightwing.

However, while Luna was progressing through the field, Askook was also closing the distance. He'd settled down, seemingly content to fly in her slipstream. But now, the big red beast put on a burst of speed while gaining altitude.

"What do you think Askook's jockey is doing?" Jackson turned to his brother.

"I don't think his jockey is doing anything but hanging on for dear life. That is one of the most ill-mannered dragons I have ever seen." Robby patted Jackson's shoulder reassuringly. "Let's just hope the big red beast is over his tantrum. If he's not, I don't think that jock can keep him from doing anything he wants."

The crowd's cheers abruptly cut off, and Jackson and Robby both jumped the barrier to sprint across the field.

CHAPTER THIRTY-SIX

DOC MILLER FINISHED RE-BANDAGING Luna's claw and stepped back to get a better overall look at the drakaina. He shook his head. "The kind of trauma dragons can withstand is truly amazing. What a crash! I still can't believe she came away with nothing worse than a broken toe and a missing claw."

"Yeah, I wish Nightwing had been so lucky. With a tear in both wings and a foot-long gash in his chest, it'll be months before he's recovered enough to start training again, let alone competing." Cullum pulled his cap off his head and rubbed his hand distractedly through his hair. "Still, we have to call ourselves lucky. That was a terrible pileup. It could've been far worse. How both jockeys survived with only cuts and bruises is nothing short of a miracle."

Jackson shuddered at the memory. Just before the wire, with a massive down-stroke of his wings, Askook intentionally knocked Luna out of the air. Her left wing folded from the blow, causing her to tumble out of control into Nightwing, taking him down with her. They both hit the ground on the far side of the finish line as Askook flew across for the win.

The only positive thing from the near tragedy was that

none of the riders or spectators received severe injuries. Both dragons were able to leave the field under their own power, and following a lengthy inquiry into the race, Askook was disqualified and placed last. The Stewards also ruled that since Luna and Nightwing had crossed the finish line with their riders still in the harness, they were awarded first and second in that order.

Jackson had collected on his bet, but there was no joy in it for him. He looked up at the sound of big diesel engines growing louder as they approached on the road to their farm.

"Those are Nolan's dragon transports. What's he doing sending them out here?" Robby asked. "I count six of them."

"We better get the halters and shanks ready." Cullum turned away as the first transport turned off the main road and started down their lane.

"What are you talking about, Da?" Jackson hurried after his father. "What's going on?"

"We've just been submarined out of our last paying client. That's what." Cullum started handing lead shanks to each of his sons. "Regan Malony is pulling all of his stock and sending them to Nolan."

"You don't know that."

"I do, Jackson." Cullum strode toward the turnaround as the first rig pulled to a stop. "It's the only explanation for those transports to be here, and since she's already out of her stall, we'll start by loading Luna."

"No, Da, we can't let this happen," Jackson grabbed his father's arm. "You have to call Mr. Malony. He can't know this is happening. He wouldn't do this to us."

"Jackson, this is happening. We won't hear from Malony until after the dragons are settled at Nolan's farm. Maybe not even then." Cullum sighed and draped his arm over Jackson's shoulder, watching the remaining trucks rumble down the lane. "It's racing, Jack. I've seen this happen before. It's just never happened to me. Can't say I like it either." He squeezed Jackson's shoulder before he walked over to greet the driver as he climbed down from the cab of the first truck in line.

CHAPTER THIRTY-SEVEN

FIVE GRIM FACES stared at the hot scones as Lorelei set the platter down. Under normal circumstances, she would have been forced to bat away five eager hands scrambling to be first. But these weren't normal circumstances.

"There's butter, jam, and clotted cream," Lorelei pointed out. Picking up the coffee pot, she went around the table, topping up mugs. Jackson still hadn't touched his milk, his drink of choice not having yet acquired a taste for the bitter brew. She found herself smiling slightly. In some ways, he was still her little boy.

"Pass the butter, Robby." Breaking the silence, Lorelei sat at the opposite end of the table from her husband and reached for a scone.

"Sure." Robby passed it down.

"Thank you," Lorelei said, splitting her scone and buttering both sides. Then she raised her eyebrows at Jackson. "Please pass the jam, Jack."

Jackson started and met her eyes. She laid a hand over his, resting on the table between them. "It's going to be all right, honey."

SHELLEY LEE RILEY • 145

"Is it?" He whispered. "I still can't believe Mr. Malony would do this to us. How many years have we trained for him?"

"A lot, twice the number of years you've been on this earth," Cullum answered.

"But why? We didn't do anything wrong. His dragons finished first and second."

"According to Regan, Nolan approached him after the race. Laying out, in fine detail, the racing landscape going forward, at least as Nolan sees it. He claims that small backwater operations like ours will not be competitive in the future. He also said that with Regan's quality of racing stock, he should be eyeing international competition. Something we can't offer him."

"But we can," Aiden interrupted.

Cullum shook his head. "We'd have to ship in for those races, putting our flyers at a disadvantage. In contrast, Nolan has operations in every country with racing venues. We can't afford to do that."

"Do you think Regan's dragons are good enough to race on that circuit?" Robby asked.

"No. No, I don't," Cullum paused. "With the possible exception of Luna, and she needs a lot of racing under her belt before she can take on that level of competition—Luna's no Nocturne. But with Nolan's help, Regan has convinced himself she is."

"Still, it's hard not to have bad feelings after the way it went down." Robby hung his head. "It just feels . . . I don't know, wrong."

"I know. But we have to accept that it's not personal. I wished Regan the best of luck and told him we'd be here if he needed anything. What else could I do?" Cullum spread his hands. "I imagine Regan's going to be hearing a lot of excuses as his dragons keep getting beat on the European circuit. I hope not. He's been a good client and friend to us.

"Because of his international footprint, Nolan has positioned himself as the dominant racing stable in our area. And it looks like he plans on showcasing some of his best flyers here. Winning all the races at the local level makes for a convincing argument when you're busily submarining the competition out of their clients.

"I won't lie to you." His gaze traveled around the table. "And I don't need to sugarcoat the situation. Times have been tough around here for some time. There's been no hiding it. But we've made it so far, and we'll find our way through this. As long as we have each other . . . and the land." Cullum made eye contact with each of his sons in turn. When his gaze settled on Lorelei, he smiled. "Family will see us through."

"Always." Lorelei smiled back and raised her mug.

"Always," Rang out around the table.

When Cullum next cleared his throat, the platter of scones was more than half empty.

"So, there's still more that we need to discuss. Nolan doesn't need Regan's six dragons or any of the others he's garnered from the farms in the area." Cullum paused and used his fork to push a crumb around his plate. "He's been systematically undermining all the racing farms since he first appeared on the scene. I think it's obvious there is more going on. It can't be about gaining more racing stock for his stable. Overall, he has better-quality dragons. Surely, Nolan doesn't need the day money. He's in the top ten worldwide rankings for races won."

"Then there are the Travellers he's allowing to camp on his land," Aiden added. "What's up with that, anyway? It's starting to look like a Travellers' convocation over there. Can any of you remember the last time one of those took place?"

"It's been decades, and never in Ireland. The last one took place in the Baltics." Brandon pushed his chair back and retrieved the coffee pot. "They like to keep them quiet, but when that many Travellers start moving and end up in one location, folk start questioning their intent."

"You boys spend enough time at the pub. Have there been any grumblings?" Lorelei asked.

"Grumbling?" Brandon laughed. "That's what race trackers do. It's always something—the soaring cost of meat, bedding, rule changes, the list is endless."

"Jockeys are always a favorite topic," Aiden piped up.

"Then there's taxes. That's always good for a grumble," Robby snorts.

"Taxes!" Cullum straightened. "That's it."

"What do you mean?" Aiden asked.

"Don't you see? It's the land Nolan wants." Cullum slapped his palm on the table. "Nolan's been trying to buy up more land since the day he arrived. So far, nobody has been willing to sell. But what happens once all the clients in the area relocate to his barn? How do any of us make a living? And when it comes down to feeding our families or paying the land taxes . . . which one do you think is going to come first?"

"Nolan bides his time, and when a farm goes under the hammer for back taxes? He'll be the only one with enough money to bid." Brandon leaned forward, his elbows on the table. "You're right, Da. That's exactly what he's up to."

"That snake." Robby pushed his chair back from the table and began to pace.

"I propose we get together with the other trainers, share our concerns, and see what their experiences with Nolan have been so far, if any." Lorelei looked around the table. "It's time all the trainers came together and devised a plan to block Nolan's takeover."

"In the meantime, we tighten our belts even further than we already have. We've got a bit saved up for a rainy day, and we still have a couple of dragons of our own who aren't too far away from a race. A little purse money would go a long way at keeping the tax man at bay."

Jackson reached into his pocket and pulled out a roll of bills. He laid it on the table.

Lorelei poked it with her finger. "Where did you get this?"

"I bet on Luna yesterday," Jackson said, pushing his winnings toward the center of the table. "I was going to buy a racing harness that I saw at the market for Tivet, but I want to contribute instead."

"We're not that desperate, Jack." Cullum sounded touched. "You keep it and spend it on whatever you want." Cullum looked around the table. "Who else bet on Luna?"

"Not me. I bet on Nightwing." Robby looked sheepish. Brandon and Aiden didn't respond.

"I did." Lorelei got up and crossed the room to the old pie cabinet in the corner. After opening a drawer, she returned to throw a large roll of bills next to Jackson's.

Cullum laughed and added his bundle to the stash.

The three older boys groaned.

"Why didn't you say something?" Brandon whined.

"Last I checked, you boyos got two eyes in your head." Cullum got up, and as he passed Jackson, he ruffled his copper curls. "That's my boy."

CHAPTER THIRTY-EIGHT

AS THEY'D DONE EACH MORNING for months, Jackson, Tivet, and Nocturne left the barn early and jogged across the fields to the far edge of the farm. Jackson knew he was being sneaky and that it was wrong. But if his family found out what he was doing, they would put a stop to it. By his way of thinking, there was only one way that he could see to help his family, and that was by being a bit reckless.

As the trio came to a stop, they stood at the edge of a small ravine that led to Lough Fad Bog. The drop into the gorge was perfect for launching without the powerful hindquarter thrust that Tivet had yet to master.

Jackson looked down at Tivet from Nocturne's greater height. The gleam of his strange scales never failed to kindle a warm thrill in Jackson's center. Tivet was so unique, so beautiful. On this morning, they reflected the vivid hues of the sunrise.

Though the dragonet was no longer small and wasn't yet big enough to ride, he wasn't far from it. His rate of growth had been nothing short of miraculous. Doc Miller said he'd never seen anything like it and upped the calcium portion to Tivet's prescribed daily supplement. The vet didn't think the feed could provide the vitamins and minerals Tivet's body needed to keep up with his phenomenal growth spurt.

~*Let's go.* Tivet spread his wings, anxious to launch. Jackson smiled at the way the dragonet's wings trembled with enthusiasm. Tivet loved to fly. He might not be able to use his hind legs to get off the ground, but once he was in the air, Tivet was unleashed lightning, rolling and darting like a leaf in a gale.

The way the dragonet buzzed around Nocturne when they were in the air, Jackson liked to compare Tivet's antics to those of a dragonfly after a mayfly.

"Hang on. I have to set my harness." Jackson tightened the straps he'd strung around Nocturne. The front strap crossed in front of her chest and ran behind Jackson's back, where he passed it through a loop he'd sewn onto his britches. The second strap went behind her forelegs and worked like a girth strap. With Jackson's knees bent, he tightened the strap in front of his ankles and over his thighs, where he'd pushed rocks to the bottom of his pockets to keep the strap in place once it was tightened. It was rudimentary and dangerous, especially with the rocks in his pockets. They would make it hard to kick out if he got in trouble. But it kept him aboard as long as Nocturne didn't decide to barrel roll in mid-air.

Though he knew how risky this cobbled-together get-up was, it wasn't like he could sneak a riding harness from the tack room without it being missed. So, for now, this rigging was going to have to do.

"Okay, I'm ready." Jackson grabbed the neck strap with both hands. "You first, Tivet."

The words were barely out of his mouth before Tivet had leapt from the ravine's edge. With his pointed wings close to his slender body, he dove, gaining speed as he plummeted. When it seemed too late to avert disaster, Tivet unfurled his wings, and with a breathtaking swoop, he twisted sharply and soared into the sky.

Every morning, as Jackson watched, he would gape in amazement. Acrobatic twists and turns, Tivet's scales flashing in the rapidly rising sun, his flight was a dance of unfettered joy, his mind-speak filled with glee.

Nocturne tightened her muscles, prepared to drop off the edge, but to Jackson's surprise, she used her powerful hindquarters for the first time since he'd started training her. Startled by her unexpected move, he fell back, the straps cutting into his flesh as Nocturne rocketed into the sky.

He yelped in fear as he experienced what a jockey must experience at the start of each race—when the dragon's power came close to overwhelming the rider's athleticism. Clinging to the neck strap, Jackson, for the first time, really understood how inadequate his makeshift harness was—exactly how significant a risk he'd been taking.

Nocturne leveled out, Jackson's heart slowed its wild beat, and he marveled, once again, at the beauty and symmetry of a racing dragon in flight. The fluidity of each downstroke, the smooth recovery, the lungs expanding with every breath. And Jackson knew he was astride the very best there'd ever been. It felt like they could fly to Africa and glide low over Stonehenge, the Eiffel Tower, and the Pyramids at Giza along the way. Jackson's heart swelled, and his confidence surged with each beat of Nocturne's wings.

We could fly around the world. Shouting a war whoop, he raised his arms overhead to fist-bump the sky.

When they swept out of the gorge and flew low over the lough's crystal-clear waters, Tivet executed a series of quick twists and turns, then, with a burst of speed, he sprinted straight for them. Nocturne glided lower, avoiding the smaller dragonet, her claws parting the water's surface. And Jackson screamed with laughter. His joy was beyond containment.

A third shadow darkened the water, and when he looked up, it was his father who looked back.

CHAPTER THIRTY-NINE

JACKSON WAITED UNTIL TIVET WAS safely on the ground before loosening the makeshift harness and sliding from Nocturne's back. Immediately, she snaked her long neck around to nuzzle Jackson, begging for attention. Feeling anxious, he rubbed Nocturne's eye ridge while he waited for his father to land.

Cullum landed his dragon at the edge of the field where Jackson's mother and brothers had gathered. Aiden stepped forward and took the reins of his father's mount.

~Where did they come from?

~They were there. You didn't notice as we landed. Jackson replied. Tivet rested his head on Jackson's shoulder.

~So, are we in trouble?

~Ya think?

~Yeah, okay, that was a stupid question. Will we be getting a whipping?

~You won't. I'm not so sure about myself, though. I've never seen Da so mad.

~He better not try anything in front of Nocturne. She might flame him.

~Tivet, you have to tell her not to do that.

Tivet had been learning the rudimentary nuances of the dragon language, and he could now, more or less, communicate with Nocturne. And at this moment, Jackson was hoping that included more than single-syllable words.

Cullum came to a stop, his gaze traveling over the trio. His eyes narrowed on the makeshift harness. Jackson didn't think he needed to worry about Nocturne flaming his da. He looked like he was about to burst into flames without any help. Cullum opened his mouth, snapping it closed several times, then turned on his heel and just walked away. Pausing before Lorelei, he pointed over his shoulder and spoke a few words before heading for the house.

~*Oh, that doesn't look good.* Tivet nudged his head under Jackson's arm.

~*No. No, it doesn't.* Jackson sighed.

His mum crossed the pasture and began to pet Nocturne.

"So, your da is pretty riled up." Lorelei scratched Nocturne under her chin. "Though I don't need to tell you that, do I?"

"No." Jackson hung his head.

"How long have you been riding Nocturne?"

"Months." Jackson tugged on his ear, his nerves getting the better of him.

"Really? Months." Lorelei moved around to get a better look at the makeshift harness. "With that?"

"Yes."

"How do you communicate with her?"

"Hands, knees, weight shifts," Nocturne nudged him. He laid his hand on her nostril, and she took a deep breath. "We understand each other."

"Jack, why wouldn't you have come to us?"

"Because you guys wouldn't have trusted me." Jackson straightened and looked his mother in the eye. "I'm no longer useless. I can do more than you know."

"Clearly, you're not useless. Nor have you ever been. Look

at what you've done with these two." She waved her hand to encompass the three of them. "But, Jack, why would you have ever considered yourself useless? No member of this family has ever believed you to be anything less than our equal.

"You are so special, I . . ." Choking on a sob, Lorelei wrapped her arms around Jackson. "My beautiful boy."

Jackson quivered in her arms. "I'm so sorry, Mum."

"Don't." Lorelei held him at arm's length. "What you did wasn't wrong, but how you went about it was. Your da is mad because you scared him half to death. He'll get over it . . . eventually." She grimaced.

CHAPTER FORTY

JACKSON ROOTED THROUGH THE patch of clover that covered the bank near the pond's edge. He and Sarah glanced up as a spray of water showered them. For the last twenty minutes, Nocturne and Tivet had been splashing in the pond, loosening a cloud of silt that clouded the water. Together, they flapped their wings, and it looked as though Nocturne might be trying to teach Tivet a water-based takeoff technique. And it was working. Almost. Tivet flapped, and his body lifted, but he couldn't quite clear the water. Still, it was progress, and Jackson thought it wouldn't be long before the dragonet took to the open skies without the aid of the drop-off.

"I was worried about you when I didn't see you at the lough." Sarah handed Jackson a four-leaf clover.

"I told you. We're grounded." Jackson cringed. "Literally."

"I know. But I didn't know that when I rode my bike out there." Digging her fingers through a mound of clover, she easily plucked another one with four leaves from the cluster.

"How do you keep finding those? I haven't found a single one." Jackson frowned at the area he'd been combing through. Sarah had been sneaking to the farm since the day they'd first met at the market. He was glad she was here with him now.

"Lucky." Sarah smiled and held it in the air. "Shall we both make a wish at the same time?"

"Why not?" Jackson laughed and held up the one she'd already given him.

"Faith," Jackson said as he plucked a leaf.

"Faith," Sarah repeated and plucked one from her stem.

"Hope." Jackson plucked another.

"Hope." Sarah followed suit.

"Friendship." Jackson squirmed as he looked at the girl before him.

"Friendship." Sarah blushed as they both pulled a leaf.

"And that leaves luck." Jackson smiled.

"Luck." Sarah smiled back, meeting his eyes. "And when you have luck, everything is possible."

"My oldest wish has already come true." Jackson held up his stem. "True friendship. You, Tivet, and Nocturne. How could I get any luckier than that?"

"You also have your family, Jackson." Sarah reached over and used the tiny green stem, with its one remaining leaf, to tap his chest. "Don't pretend that they don't count. No matter what, they'll always love you. My mum loved me, and she was my best friend," She rolled her lips before continuing. "And then she was gone."

"Where did she go?"

"She died," Sarah murmured, swirling the clover stem between her thumb and forefinger. You don't get to return from that, no matter how much love you had for the ones you left behind." Her gaze shifted to the two dragons; their wings spread, floating across the water. "I was sent to live with my father, who hates me. Toby, my half-brother, hates me even more. The Travellers say I'm a bad omen and that I brought *mí-ádh* with me. They all call me Wraith." She dropped the green stem back onto the patch it had come from, a wry twist to her lips. "But then you and Tivet came along, and you didn't care what I looked like or where I came from." When she raised her eyes, they were filled with unshed tears. "And if I disappeared, I think you're the only one who would wonder or care."

"That can't be true. Surely, they would look for you if you didn't come home."

"Jackson, they wouldn't even notice I was gone. How do you think I have gotten away with coming here so often?"

He stared at the small girl in disbelief. He knew his family loved him, even though they recognized Jackson was damaged. And if he was honest with himself, he knew his father's current anger was because he cared.

Unsure what he could say, Jackson picked up the clover she'd discarded. With the one he still held, he placed both on her palm and curled her fingers over.

"You and me, Sarah." Jackson placed his other hand over hers. "Double the luck."

Slapping his wings on the water, Tivet propelled himself from the pond, spraying Jackson and Sarah.

~Hey, don't forget about me.

CHAPTER FORTY-ONE

"WHERE IS THAT GIRL? WHEN I find her, I'm going to tan her hide." Lash growled. "Maybe she's run off to be with her mother's kin. I wish I could see Sarah's face when she learns that foul woman refused to take her own granddaughter in after her mother died. I think she refused just to spite me."

"The reason that hag didn't want her was because Sarah's a freak." Toby poked a stick into the campfire and watched as the flames licked at the tip and the wood began to smoke. "Snooping around, listening in where she don't belong. Nobody likes her. Why don't we dump her in a village and let the government take her?"

"Don't think I haven't considered it," Lash said, pulling a beer out of the cooler beside his camp chair and popping the tab.

"So why didn't you?"

"My *máthair*," Lash said, taking a big swig of the foamy brew. "That woman's gone soft, Toby. Next, she'll want us to go to Sunday service."

Toby snickered. "Ya Ya did say something like that the last time you got drunk."

"Yeah? Well, maybe it's past time I reminded her who wears the pants around here."

"She does." Toby laughed, ducking out of reach of Lash's fist.

"Watch your mouth, punk." Lash stared into the center of the fire. "When's the last time you went out to collect a bounty? The money from the last one is running out."

"Trust me, I've tried. But they've been sending outriders to patrol while their dragons are training."

"Excuses." Lash jabbed a finger in Toby's direction. "I never thought I'd live to see the day when a son of mine would turn into a sniffling coward. Are you sure you're even my son?" Lash knew Toby wasn't a coward. But with each beer that disappeared down his gullet, Lash's desire to badger his boy grew stronger. And tonight's drinking had started mid-afternoon.

"But Da."

"Don't you dare 'but Da' me." Lash surged to his feet, swaying as he loomed over his son. "We don't get paid for watching dragons train. You put a hole in two dragon wings tomorrow, or you and I will come to an understanding before the entire tribe in the clearing. Might do some good for these whiney little mama's boys running around camp. They need a reminder about how a *real* Traveller can take a whooping like a man."

Lash threw his head back and emptied the can of beer before tossing it into the fire. A car pulled off the road, briefly illuminating their surroundings before the headlights extinguished.

"Make yourself useful." Lash used the toe of his boot to push Toby off the stump he'd been perched on. To Lash's way of thinking, messing with Toby was part of his job; how else was the knucklehead supposed to learn what it meant to be a man? "Find more beer." Lash smirked as Toby scrambled to his feet and hurried away. *A real man like his da.* Smiling at the thought, Lash turned to greet his visitor.

While Lash had been expecting a visit, eventually, it wasn't from the man who climbed out of the car.

"Lash."

"Connor." Lash made an effort to disguise his surprise. Connor Doyle was not someone Lash would have thought to see in his camp. "What brings you to my fire?"

"The boss sent me." Connor was a big man, broad in the chest with powerful arms. And at the moment, his demeanor was far from friendly. Clenching his fists, he looked like he badly wanted to use them on Lash.

"Now you don't say. Why would 'the boss' be sending the likes of you my way?" Too drunk to resist taunting the belligerent man. "I thought he liked keeping his sheep in the sheepfold."

It was no secret to the Travellers that as a longtime member of the local dragon racing community, Connor had been hired by Duffy Nolan to run his new farm. He'd done it for a reason, and it had nothing to do with Connor's abilities. Connor was a drunk and a gambler, both vices contributing to his downfall. But Lash knew Connor punched the ticket for Duffy. Putting a local into the position would blunt any suspicions aimed at Duffy as he implemented his plan to control the entire region. Duffy also wanted a haven from the prying eyes of his detractors on the European mainland.

CHAPTER FORTY-TWO

CULLUM, MOUNTED ON THE FARM'S lead dragon, waited in the grassy area by the pond for Jackson to bring the glistening black dragon to a stop. Cullum had instructed him to put the tack on Nocturne and bring her to the launching pad.

As Cullum watched the trio's approach, he found it challenging to maintain a cool reserve. Tivet was feeling frisky, jumping on Nocturne's tail before bucking and romping out of the way as she switched it in his direction. As for the beautiful dragon, she was also on the muscle. Her wings, while not furled, neither were they clasped close to her body. With her neck arched, she pranced sideways, the blue-black sheen of her scales rippling as the early morning light caressed her sleek body.

A training harness strapped to her back meant one thing to Nocturne—flight. And there was no doubt she was anxious to take to the air. Cullum caught his breath as Tivet suddenly launched into the air, and Nocturne reared in response, anxious to follow him.

When did the dragonet gain enough strength to launch from a standing start? To Cullum, it felt like another oversite on his part. He'd been so engrossed in his problems that he failed to see what was happening in his own backyard.

"Steady." As Jackson spoke to Nocturne, he let the lead shank run through his hands. Locking up on the leather strap would have only pulled him off his feet and under Nocturne's sharp claws. Cullum nodded his approval but didn't comment. He didn't want Jackson to think he was surprised at how well he handled the excited dragon. The boy would only see it as a criticism.

Besides, he was still mad at Jackson for putting himself in danger by riding Nocturne without first seeking approval and minus the proper equipment. Whenever Cullum was reminded of what could have happened to his boy, his stomach plunged and reignited his anger. Then there was the whole trust issue, and that wasn't helping. Hiding that he'd been riding Nocturne spotlighted the biggest problem for Cullum—Jackson knew what he was doing was wrong. It was deceitful, not a word he would have ever considered using in the same sentence with his son. But he had used it and knew it had hurt Jackson to hear it. But it had to be said.

"Get control of your dragonet, Jackson." Cullum pointed at Tivet, who was currently doing a series of barrel rolls overhead. *And how the heck is that wee beast doing that anyway?* "If anyone gets hurt due to his antics, he'll be confined to his stall during training hours."

"How's he going to stop him?" Robby laughed as he joined them.

Jackson put two fingers in his mouth and let rip a shrill whistle as he glared at Robby.

"Sorry, Jack," Robby said. "I didn't mean it like that."

"What else did you mean?" Jackson spat as Tivet dove from the sky and failed to back-wing until crashing head-first into the ground appeared inevitable. Jackson held his breath until Tivet executed a maneuver that would have been hard to describe and safely landed. "Creature deaf? Only good for shoveling scat? You don't have to say it out loud, Robby."

"That's enough, Jackson," Cullum snapped. "Robby, let's go. Mount up."

Jackson unsnapped the lead shank from the bridle ring, Robby gathered the reins, and as Jackson reached to give Robby a leg up onto Nocturne's back, she sidled away. Jackson followed along, grabbing Robby's calf as he jumped, giving him a boost onto the dragon's back.

With Robby firmly settled, Nocturne froze. Cullum could see Robby trying to communicate with his mount, but it quickly became apparent that she wouldn't obey. Shaking her head, Nocturne sank to the ground.

"What's wrong, Robby?" Cullum shifted in the riding harness, preparing to dismount.

"I don't know. I know she's listening." Robby dropped the reins and slid from her back. "But she's refusing to respond." Nocturne instantly rose and snaked her head around to nuzzle Jackson. "Well, that's interesting."

Cullum slid from his mount's back and approached Nocturne. He ran his hand over her face, and she rubbed an eye ridge against his chest.

"Give me a leg up, Robby." Cullum gathered the reins and indicated that Jackson should step aside. "And get Tivet out of the way. I'm not going to warn you again."

Before Cullum could settle his feet in the stirrups, Nocturne sank back to the ground. Cullum dropped the reins, resting his hands on his thighs for a moment before he shook his head and climbed down.

"Did she communicate with you?" Robby asked.

"Oh yes. The image she sent was quite clear." Cullum turned to look at his youngest son.

"Jackson? She wants Jackson?" Robby stared at his brother, who sat on the ground over by the barn watching the proceedings with Tivet's head on his lap. "He can't ride her."

"Oh, yes, he can. I'm sure you recall that fact as well as I do." Cullum shoved his hands into his pockets. Turning his face to the sky, he closed his eyes. Seconds passed before he took a deep breath and turned to speak to Jackson. "Put these dragons away, then come to the house."

"Family meeting?" Robby asked.

"You might call it that," Cullum said over his shoulder as he strode away.

CHAPTER FORTY-THREE

JACKSON RAN a rub rag over Nocturne; his brow creased with worry. He knew why Nocturne refused to obey both Robby and his father. As hard as it was to believe, she wanted him as her jockey, creature deaf Jackson.

Tivet had explained it to Jackson while he was removing the tack from Nocturne, and nothing Jackson could say would change her mind.

Knuckling his tired eyes, he headed for the house. How would he explain this to his da without giving away the secret he shared with Tivet? Maybe it's time to come clean, he'd told Tivet. But the little dragonet would have none of it, melting into a quivering mass at the suggestion. Which, of course, served to rile up Nocturne to the point that she began huffing smoke through her nostrils.

It had taken a goodly amount of convincing to calm them both down. So now Jackson was late and undoubtedly in trouble, yet again. Sighing, he ran his hands through his hair before opening the back door and stopping in the mudroom to remove his Wellies. He could hear the clink of silverware in the other room, and an ominous lack of conversation.

Hesitating in the doorway to the kitchen, he stared as a cold finger of dread trailed over his skin. Five solemn faces were focused on him.

"I'm glad you decided to join us." Cullum broke the silence before continuing to stir the contents of his cup.

"I'm sorry, Da. Nocturne was upset, and it took a while to get her to settle down."

"That's understandable. She's full of fire and needs to fly." Cullum crossed his arms over his chest.

Anxiety hung like a heavy shroud over the room. If Jackson could have sunk into the floor, he would have done so willingly.

"Too bad there isn't anyone sitting at this table who can do that. Isn't that right?"

"It's . . ." Jackson began. It wasn't like there was anything he could say in response.

"Don't start, Jack." Cullum raised his hand. "You don't get to say this isn't your fault because it is."

"Now, wait a minute," Lorelei interrupted, pushing back her chair; she closed the distance to lay her arm over her son's shoulder. Pulling him close, she locked gazes with her husband. "You told Jackson . . . no, the truth of it is that you challenged him to save that dragon." She looked down into Jackson's tear-filled eyes.

"And he did," she whispered. Cupping Jackson's chin in her hand, her eyes also glistened with unshed tears. "I am so proud of you, *mo chróí*. You did what the rest of us could not. In my opinion, you saved the bravest and most beautiful dragon that has ever been born."

Lorelei turned her gaze to the rest of the family. "I don't want to hear any more of this. We owe Jackson more than we can ever express in words. He certainly doesn't deserve any blame. Besides, placing blame is counterproductive. Let's spend our time coming up with a solution for our current predicament." Her eyes locked with Cullum's. "While you were storming around in a temper, did you happen to consider Jackson may have, single-handedly, given us a way to save the farm?"

"That's right!" Brandon whooped, surging to his feet, the chair he'd been sitting in scraping loudly against the floor. "If Nocturne can fly, then she can race."

Cullum's eyes narrowed. "And just who's going to ride her? If she won't fly for one of us, she certainly won't launch for a jockey."

"Jackson." Robby rose to stand beside Brandon in solidarity. "He can ride her."

"I second that," Brandon agreed.

"As do I," Aiden's voice joined in. "He's certainly the right size. He'll be the lightest rider out there."

"Well, there you have it." Lorelei grinned. "Jackson, it is. Problem solved."

Jackson couldn't believe what he was hearing. He looked at his da and wasn't encouraged by what he saw. The feelings that flashed across Cullum's face were, in parts, astonishment and disbelief, but the emotion that stood out from the rest was fear.

"He doesn't know how to fly." Cullum sat forward in his seat.

"He does," Lorelei countered. "Isn't that what this meeting was all about?"

"Lorelei, get serious." Cullum waved his hand to encompass Jackson. "He may be able to cling to a harness, but he doesn't have the experience to ride Nocturne against a field of top-notch dragons guided by veteran jockeys. He wouldn't stand a chance. Besides, who wants to address the real fire-breathing dragon in the room? Hmmm?"

Cullum looked around. "Anybody? Come on. I'm listening."

"Stop it! Don't make them say it." Jackson stepped away from his mother. "Why don't you say it, Da? You're thinking it. I'm creature deaf. No one would allow me to ride in a race."

Jackson raced from the room, grabbed his Wellies, and stuttered-stepped to put them on one at a time as he rushed away from the house. He didn't stop until he stood before Nocturne's stall, where the black dragon and Tivet waited.

He gasped for air as he stared through the bars. Feeling unworthy, he didn't roll back the gate.

~*What's wrong?* Tivet sounded scared.

~*You deserve better. You both deserve better than me.*

Jackson turned and jogged away.

~*No! Don't go. Don't leave me.* Tivet trumpeted his fear into Jackson's thoughts.

~*I'm sorry.*

Jackson ran, and Nocturne's roars only spurred him to run faster.

CHAPTER FORTY-FOUR

IT WASN'T UNTIL THE STITCH IN HIS SIDE became unendurable that Jackson slowed to a stop. Bent over and gasping for air, he stared into the slow-moving creek that burbled along the far border of his family's land.

Sun dabbled the water's surface, and silver fingerlings flicked through the shallows. Collapsing on the grassy bank, Jackson drew his knees to his chest.

Resting his chin on his knees, his gaze wandered over the verdant croft the dragon farms shared when training their flyers. But at the moment, he didn't see the beauty in the scene. It was the image of the five disappointed faces that filled his mind. He didn't listen to the cheerful bird song or the soft murmur the water made as it traveled over the rocks. He remembered the sound of Nocturne's roars—the terror in Tivet's pleas.

And I just ran away!

Time slipped by, and as it did, Jackson's guilt and self-doubt worsened. What could he do? Until Tivet came along, hope seemed like a concept that stayed well beyond his reach. And now, even that had been taken from him. He'd helped

Nocturne recover, only to make her, if anything, more useless than she'd been while injured. They would lose the farm, and it would be his fault.

"Jackson," a panic-filled voice penetrated his pity party. "Jackson, please, you've got to do something."

Jackson looked to where Sarah scrambled across the pasture on the far side of the creek. Once she got his attention, she waved her arms frantically, a brightly colored scarf clutched in her hand.

Jackson jumped to his feet. Panic gripped him when she tripped and failed to rise. Using a familiar set of stepping stones, he quickly reached the far bank and raced to where the small girl lay sobbing in the grass.

"Are you hurt?"

Sarah raised a tear-stained face, her eyes filled with fear. "Toby's going to do something awful. Please, we have to stop him!"

Chapter Forty-Five

GREBES, DUMPY BIRDS, WITH their stupid wit-wit calls, took flight as Toby limped along a soggy sliver of land that wound through the tall reeds. When his injured leg suddenly gave way, he ended up on his hands and knees in the muck. Cursing under his breath, he used his bow to lever himself back to his feet.

Taking the time to adjust the strap on his quiver and recover the scattered arrows. Toby reflected on the worst beating his da had given him in a long while. Drunker, and more belligerent following Connor Doyle's visit, Lash had hunted Toby down. While he was well used to the switch and his father's fists, bone-bruising kicks were a new form of punishment and the cause of Toby's painful limp.

But there was no time for whinging. He had a job to do, and if he failed, there'd be worse in store for him. Lash had no tolerance for excuses. Toby felt a wave of nausea at the thought of what that might look like—feel like.

Pushing aside the tall reeds, he peered into the sky. Connor hadn't beat around the bush, relaying Duffy's message in two sentences. Lash would stick to the bargain they'd struck or else. And Duffy wanted a shiny black dragon to fall afoul of one of Toby's well-aimed arrows.

It didn't matter who this dragon was nor why it was important to Duffy that it be taken down. Toby would shoot a hole through its wing, and the way he was feeling today, maybe both wings. If the arrows could've penetrated their scales, he would have shot to kill every one of the flying lizards he'd already maimed for Duffy. But that wasn't what the man wanted. It would bring too much attention.

Bring too much attention? Toby snarled at the thought. Toby already had their attention. After the second time he'd put a hole in a wing, the dragon trainers had sent outriders with their beasts.

With a hooded jacket the same color as the reeds that stood twice his height. He felt certain that the outriders would never spot him, even if they flew directly overhead. And they would; this was the dragons' route to and from the training area.

As he settled in to wait, Toby looked around and considered moving to another section of the wetlands that bordered the lough. The path he'd made out to the point had become too obvious. He sighed. *Not today.* His knee was too sore to beat a new path. He pushed aside his unease at being spotted. As it was, once the arrow was shot, he didn't need to add distance to his getaway.

Toby didn't have long to wait. The beat of massive wings displacing the air was unmistakable. Readying himself, he raised his bow, arrow nocked in place. He only had a short window to identify his target and get the shot off before the reeds obscured his view.

The shadow cast by an enormous body raced toward Toby's hiding spot. He pulled back the string, readying his aim. With one eye closed, he noted the dark black scales of the dragon that flew into view. It must be the one. He lowered his aim to catch the dragon's downswing, making it less likely that the rider would notice the projectile. They wouldn't see the injury until they'd returned to the farm.

"I'm telling you there's a path right here."

Startled by his sister's voice, Toby jerked as the bowstring twanged with the release. He knew his arrow wouldn't fly true, but more importantly, he was about to be discovered.

A sharp yelp of pain from overhead covered any sound Toby made as he slipped into the water, abandoning his weapon.

"You there! Stay where you are." A gruff voice yelled from the back of a red dragon. The beast hovered right above where Toby had been standing. With his heart in his throat, he sank further into the mud-stained water.

As backwash from the ginormous wings flattened the mud-stained reeds, it exposed Sarah and that little curly-haired rotter she was so in love with. Toby smirked at the irony. Possibly, the two people he hated most in the world, the ones who had thought to catch him in the act, were the ones caught—the evidence of their crime lying in the mud at their feet.

Chapter Forty-Six

"Da, I'm telling you that it wasn't us. It was Toby!" Jackson jumped up from the plain wooden bench where he and Sarah sat, his features twisted in anger.

Both of Jackson's parents were standing in the headquarters of the local Garda Síochána. For their small village, this consisted of two rooms added onto the side of the building which housed the volunteer fire brigade. The bland interior held little besides a desk, three chairs, and the rickety bench where they sat. In contrast, the other room contained only a holding cell with the customary iron-barred door.

"Sit down, Jackson," Cullum snapped. "You'll get your chance to speak."

"But, Da." Jackson was beside himself. *How can this be happening?*

"That's enough!" Cullum pointed at the bench. "I won't repeat myself."

Jackson sat next to the softly weeping Sarah. He reached out and took her hand. She leaned into him, her tears quickly dampening his sleeve.

"It's gonna be okay. My da will find the truth of it."

Jackson tried to sound reassuring.

"Start over, Rory. Jackson won't be interrupting us again." Cullum gave Jackson a warning look.

"Well, as I was saying. Connor Doyle was out flying with Harris Flynn, who was riding Nightwing." Rory tugged on the collar of his slightly rumpled uniform. "You do remember Nightwing? Don't you, Cullum?"

"Of course I do. We both know he's coming back from an injury. Stop acting the maggot, Rory. What happened, and why is my son and this wee lass sitting in your office like a couple of hardened criminals?"

"Harris Flynn was shot in the leg with an arrow. And your son was found standing over these." The dark-haired Garda gestured at the mud-stained bow and quiver resting on his desk. "Quite literally right after it happened."

Cullum barked out a laugh devoid of humor. Pointing at the bow, he stated. "You think my boy could draw that bow? It's longer than he is tall. And those arrows, look at the tip. It would take someone with more strength than Jackson has in his entire body to shoot an arrow that heavy, let alone with any accuracy. You need to look elsewhere for your villain, Rory."

"Cullum, I'm telling you Jackson was found mere seconds after Harris was wounded, and he was standing over these very items. Nobody else was in the vicinity at the time of the attack." He gestured toward Sarah. "Neither of us is going to point the finger at her, are we?" Despite Rory's words, Jackson was thrilled to see the first inklings of doubt cross the Garda's features.

Lorelei, who'd stayed silent up to that point, stepped forward. Picking up the bow, she hefted it and fingered the string. "I think a straightforward demonstration can prove my child's innocence."

"Mum! I am not a child." The look Lorelei shot Jackson was far more effective at shutting him up than any of his father's harsh words.

"Here, Rory, try drawing this bowstring yourself." Leaning over the desk, she offered the bow to the Garda.

While Rory didn't overly struggle to draw the bowstring, it was evident that it took a good deal of strength, and that was without a heavy arrow notched in place. Rory looked at Jackson as he laid the bow back on the desk. He shook his head. "You're right. He couldn't have done it. So, what am I supposed to do, Cullum? They were right there, nobody else."

"Maybe you should drag Toby and Lash in for a natter. You might get to the bottom of this."

The door crashed against the wall as Lash Coffey stormed into the building.

"What is going on in here?" Lash elbowed Lorelei, none too gently, out of his way to confront Rory. "Who gave you the right to drag my daughter in here without contacting me first?"

Jackson surged to his feet as Cullum shoved Lash. "You watch who you're pushing around, you good-for-nothing sod."

Lash turned, fists ready as the two men squared off.

"Here now, we'll have none of that." Rory hustled around the desk to separate the two men.

Lorelei stepped in front of Jackson, which was a good thing as Toby hustled through the door and made a beeline for him.

"You stand down." Lorelei pointed a finger at Toby. "We'll have none of your mischief today."

"That's his bow and arrows." Jackson leaned around to point at Toby.

"And what if they are?" Toby crossed his thick arms over his broad chest.

"Are you admitting these items are yours?" Rory looked at Toby.

"Yes, and she stole them." He pointed at Sarah, who cringed under his baleful glare.

"She did not." Jackson pushed against his mother's hold. "You're a liar!"

"Prove it," Toby smirked.

"Where were you this morning?" Rory narrowed his eyes at the smug teenager.

"He was with me all morning," Lash replied for his son. "He hasn't left my sight. Are you planning on telling me what this is all about?"

"Somebody used that bow and shot an arrow just like these," he pointed at the quiver, "into Harris Flynn, who was flying one of Regan Malony's dragons at the time. Do you know anything about that?"

"No, I don't. Besides, what would be my motivation for injuring anyone or anything associated with Duffy Nolan? My clan's camped on his land." Lash turned to Cullum and curled his lip as he raked his eyes over the smaller man. "On the other hand, it would seem Cullum here and his get have at least six good reasons to want revenge on Duffy. Why don't you ask Cullum where *he* was this morning?"

Rory turned his gaze on Cullum.

"Seriously? You'd listen to this piece of . . ."

Lorelei cleared her throat before her husband could finish. "He was with me . . ." She smirked at Lash. "All morning. We were cleaning the chicken coop." She strolled over and plucked a red chicken feather from Cullum's collar.

Rory rolled his eyes, circled his desk, and sat down. "We're getting nowhere. You can all leave. But don't think for one minute I'm letting this drop. A man was injured. And somehow, amongst the lot of you, I believe one of you knows exactly what happened out there."

Toby limped over and reached for his bow and quiver.

"Leave it. It's evidence." Rory opened a drawer, pulled out a couple of evidence tags, and began to write. He looked up, his gaze clashing with Lash. "Don't leave the district, Lash."

"Don't you worry yourself none," Lash sneered. "I got plenty of reasons to stick around." He grabbed Sarah by the upper arm and dragged her off the bench. Jackson clung to her hand.

"You wanna let go of her before I make you." Lash towered over Jackson.

"Don't threaten my son, Lash. You'll regret it."

"I told your pup to stay away from Sarah, but he don't listen any better than his da."

"Enough." Rory's swivel chair groaned as he stood. "I told you to leave, Lash. If you two start anything in here, you'll be finishing it in there." Rory pointed toward the holding cell. "Anybody *want* to test my resolve?"

Lash and Toby, with Sarah in tow, left, leaving the door open behind them.

"Da, he's going to hurt Sarah. We have to do something."

"There's nothing your father can do," Rory answered for Cullum. "Just for the record, did Sarah steal these?" He pointed to the items he was tying the tags to.

"No. They were lying in the mud when we got there."

"And why exactly were you there?" Rory asked.

"Sarah came to me, and she was crying. She said that Toby was going to do something bad. Then she showed me where she thought he was headed. When we got there, Toby was gone, and these," Jackson pointed at the weapon, "were lying in the mud, and Toby was nowhere around. He must have hidden in the water. That's all I can think of. Where else could he have gone in so little time?"

"All right. Go on home, Cullum. I know Jackson couldn't have done this, but I'm not sure we'll be able to convince Duffy Nolan of that."

"I'm not sure Nolan wasn't the one behind this. Are you?"

There was no reply as Cullum led the way to the old farm pickup parked at the curb.

Jackson knew that Rory wasn't paid to make assumptions. He'd been hired to find the truth and uphold the law. Still, that knowledge didn't make the situation any less frustrating. Something terrible was in the offing, and Jackson was afraid there was no way his family would be able to avoid the fallout.

CHAPTER FORTY-SEVEN

THE EYE OF THE DRAGON HAD served as the community center for decades and was where Jackson and his family were headed. His da parked in the grassy area next to the pub, and as Jackson looked around, he was amazed at the number of vehicles that had arrived before them. Clamoring from the bed of the pick-up truck with his brothers, they joined their parents as they walked toward a squat, white-washed building sporting a newly thatched roof.

More than a week had passed since he and Sarah were discovered in the reeds with Toby's bow and arrows lying at their feet. Naturally, at first, it was assumed they'd been responsible for the injury to Harris, the jockey. With the bow far too big for either Jackson or Sarah to wield, Garda Rory had to admit they were not guilty of the act. But despite Rory's continued efforts, he hadn't found evidence to tie Toby to the crime.

As they often did, Jackson's thoughts turned to Sarah. After Lash forcibly dragged the weeping girl from the Garda Síochána, Jackson hadn't heard from her. Lash was a brute, and even though it was Jackson who'd pointed the finger, there was little doubt Sarah would be blamed for the accusation lodged against Toby.

As for her brother, it didn't take a genius to understand that the boy was a product of his upbringing. Subjugating those he felt were inferior, which was just about anybody smaller or younger. Toby was a bully.

Not knowing how his friend fared was driving Jackson crazy. Icy fingers of dread were his constant companion. But his parents warned that if they tried to intervene, it would only make things worse. Without obvious signs of abuse, the law was on Lash's side.

"Looks like we're going to have a good turnout," Cullum said, greeting a group of trainers gathered at the front of the picnic area beside the pub. Brightly colored red and white umbrellas and checkered vinyl tablecloths were a cheerful invitation for customers to sit at one of the half-dozen wooden picnic tables. While the weather remained warm enough to gather outside, the meeting was scheduled to be held inside the pub.

"More than you might expect, Cullum." Shamus Smyth, a longtime resident, pointed toward the road. Everyone stared as a sleek black limousine came to a stop. A tinted window slowly lowered. And there sat the very man that everyone was there to discuss. Duffy Nolan. In the flesh, with a smug look planted firmly on his handsome face. Dark wavy hair topped heavy eyebrows and a pair of icy-blue eyes that he turned on the gathering.

This was the first time Jackson had seen Duffy in person. Too slick to the point of being slimy, it wasn't just Duffy's looks that raised the tiny hairs on the back of Jackson's neck. Something dark and primitive lurked in the depths of those blue eyes. This man was a predator.

"Evening, gentlemen. A glorious late summer's eve, wouldn't you agree?" Not one among them deigned to answer.

But judging by Duffy's tone, Jackson didn't think the man expected a response.

"Well . . . considering the lack of cordiality, should I assume I'm not welcome to this meeting of Irish dragon folk?"

"You're not one of us, *Duffy*," Shamus said, making no attempt to disguise his resentment. Jackson fidgeted. With so much anger on display, he didn't see how this confrontation could help but boil over.

"You don't say? Then what does that make me?" Duffy's smile had turned wolfish.

"The enemy." A voice called from what was quickly becoming a crowd as more people left the pub to see what was going on.

"Is that the way of it then?" Duffy tilted his head, waiting for an affirmation that didn't come. "All right." He nodded as if in agreement. "Then let me impart a word of advice. Before starting a war with me, you should consider if there is even one among you who has what it takes to win such a war?" His disdainful gaze raked over Cullum. With a dismissive wave of his hand, the limousine pulled away.

INSIDE THE DRAGON EYE, unease settled like a shroud over the village folk crowding the pub's interior. Far from the friendly and casual atmosphere he'd come to expect, the building's dark wood interior and low lighting seemed diminished. The polished brass dragon medallions that lined the wooden beams appeared less lustrous. The stone hearth, where a cauldron of stew hung during the cold winter months, was a dank, stone-lined hole in the wall without the warmth a flickering fire brought. Jackson, not unaffected by the atmosphere, claimed a seat between Robby and Aiden.

The murmuring that buzzed in the background gained in

volume as Cullum moved to stand before the podium. He cleared his voice and waited until the only sound that remained was the quiet rustle of clothing as the pub's occupants settled.

"I want to start by saying we're not here to discuss what has been happening in our community."

"Well, what the *ifrinn* are we here for?" A gravelly voice called from the back of the room.

"Calm yourself, Jamison." Another voice rose over the sudden flurry of chatter. "Let the man speak."

"We all know what's been going on. We don't need to waste our time nattering on about it." Cullum spoke into the expectant hush. "We need to talk about what *we'll* do about it. And I say, before we can do anything, we must first find the answer to a one-word question. Why? Why is the all-mighty Duffy Nolan, Europe's leading trainer, doing this? What is his motivation for bankrupting every dragon trainer in the valley? What's in it for him? We are not his competition. And with very few exceptions, none of the clients he's submarined have dragons that could compete on the European circuit. If we don't know the why, how will we fight back?" Cullum glanced around the room to pause on specific individuals. "Any thoughts?"

Jackson scooted around in his seat, craning his neck to identify who his father targeted. Usually, these were the more outspoken members of the community. But not today. Those sat with clouded expressions, their arms crossed tightly over their chests—a defensive posture Jackson was quite familiar with.

Cullum seemed content to let the silence drag on. The night before, he'd informed the family that though it always fell to him to lead the discussion at these meetings, he wouldn't this time. Every family affected needed to put their own interests aside and work together as a community.

Without a cohesive front, it was clear that Duffy Nolan, with all his resources, would continue to pick them off one at a time.

"I don't know the answer to why Duffy is doing what he's doing." Shamus stood up, twisting his cap as he spoke. "Other than the obvious. If he bankrupts each and every one of us, he can buy our land for halfpennies on the pound. All he has to do is wait. When we can't pay our tax bill, and our holdings go under the hammer, he'll be the only one bidding . . ." His voice trailed off. "My bill is already past due."

"I'm sorry to hear that, Shamus." Cullum grimaced. "You're not alone in this predicament, which is why we're here. Let's put our heads together and come up with some ideas."

"I don't know about suggestions." Shamus remained standing, his posture straightening. "But I called my cousin Flynn in Paris last night, and he had much to say about Duffy Nolan. The most relevant of which is that Nolan's spending time in Ireland because he's been ruled off for doping his flyers. Until his suspension is up, he's not allowed to set foot on any of the European race tracks."

"Doping?" Outraged voices rang out around the room.

"That's right. And not only that, there are race-fixing allegations." Shamus paused, lowering his voice. "Whispers are going around that he's gone and got himself mixed up with the mob."

Jackson gasped. *The mob?* Lorelei reached across the table to cover his hand. Her quiet reassurance helped with the surge of fear the word engendered. Everybody knew about the mob. It was in all the papers. The mob had their fingerprints on all sorts of criminal activities.

"Those are some bloody big allegations. Is there any proof to support these rumors?" Someone called out. Jackson didn't recognize the voice.

"Well, Flynn said that a dragon, the favorite, mind you, showed up with acid burns on his back the morning of the race he was scheduled to fly. As you can well imagine, he was scratched from the race. Another instance was a dragon who showed up, also a favorite, in the saddling paddock showing signs of having been tranquilized—again, scratched. And there have been several cases of tainted meat being tossed into stalls at night. Resulting in further scratches."

"Any witnesses?" Cullum voiced what Jackson was thinking.

"None. But does it matter when Duffy Nolan's dragons won every race where the favorite was scratched? It's a rather convenient coincidence, don't you think?"

"What are the local officials doing about it?" Lorelei joined the conversation.

"Nothing. Flynn says it's an ill-kept secret that the mob has been buying a lot of cooperation. He even believes there are jockeys being paid to put the arm on their mounts."

"What does that mean?" Jackson whispered to Robby.

"It's a euphuism for influencing their mount not to perform to its best ability. With dragon speak, who could tell? Which is why it's better if you have a jockey in the family." Robby waggled his eyebrows. "Lucky, we have you."

Jackson snorted.

And that's all it took for them to get *the look* from their mum.

CHAPTER FORTY-EIGHT

A SNAP OF CALLUSED FINGERS got Jackson's attention. With another week without any news from Sarah, he could think of little else, even when being addressed at a family meeting.

"Wake up, squirt." Robby poked Jackson in the ribs. "You might want to listen."

"Don't call me that." Jackson snapped at his brother. "You know I don't like it, and that's why you do it."

"Whoa. I meant nothing by it." Robby leaned back, hands in the air. "What's got into you anyway? You're tetchier than a Kraken with a mast stuck in his craw."

"That's enough, you two." Cullum slapped his hand on the table. "I need you to pay attention to what I have to say. It affects us all, and I'm afraid it's not good news."

Jackson straightened. Nobody in the family had been particularly jovial for some time. But the grimness reflected on his da's face was unnerving. Jackson looked at Lorelei, who sat staring at the remains of the dinner she'd barely touched. When she looked up, it was evident Lorelei dreaded what was about to be said.

"I won't drag this out," his da sighed. "You've all known

for quite some time that money has been tight, and it has only gotten worse with the loss of Malony's dragons—much worse."

"We'll tighten our belts," Brandon interrupted. "I can get an outside job."

"We can all get a job," Aiden piped in. "With so few dragons left on the farm, it's not like we're needed here full-time."

"Even if people were hiring, and they're not, the other farms are in worse shape than ours. It still wouldn't be enough." Cullum gave Aiden's shoulder a quick squeeze. "But your mum and I thank you, all of you, for the offer."

Lorelei pushed away from the table and retreated to her safe zone—the green enameled Aga, where she spent the greater part of each day creating the meals her family enjoyed. Grabbing a towel, she pulled two pies from the oven. Apple, Jackson guessed if the sweet and fruity smell was anything to go by.

"Spit it out, Da," Robby exclaimed. "We can't help if we don't know what has brought you to your knees."

Jackson was shocked at Robby's bluntness. It was unthinkable to insinuate that their father was surrendering. Where Lorelei was their rock, Cullum was their fortress. The bad guys could never get in while Cullum guarded the gate. His mum remained before the Aga, her back to the discussion.

"I wish it was as simple as standing up to a challenge, Robby." Cullum shook his head sadly and glanced at his wife's stiff posture before continuing. "But I'm afraid this is not a fight we can win. Taxes are due in six months, and we won't have the money. The feed bill came in yesterday." He pulled a thickly folded piece of paper from his pocket and tossed it to the middle of the table for everyone to see. "The bills will keep coming. Feed, insurance, utilities, groceries, health care, vet bills, and . . . there will always be more. Things happen, flat tires, broken fencing, burst pipes, and those repairs never come free. While part-time jobs will help with the bills, they won't solve the larger problem of land taxes. I'm afraid to say it, but the time has come to admit the inevitable. We're going to lose the farm."

"What? No. This can't happen." Jackson surged to his feet. It was as if his father's words had sucked all the warmth from the room. "What are we going to do?"

"We sell Nocturne."

Lorelei thunked a pie down in the center of the table. Straightening, hands on her hips, she directed her gaze around the table, engaging each of her sons until she stopped on that of her husband.

"Or . . . we let Nocturne fly." She challenged.

CHAPTER FORTY-NINE

LASH'S RESENTMENT INCREASED the closer he got to Duffy's home, if the building could be called that. To say the old farmhouse had been updated was a laugh. Little remained of the simple gable-ended farmhouse Lash and his tribe had passed in their travels back when he was little more than a lad. If anything remained of the original dwelling, it was buried deep within the *teach mór* that now stood in its place.

The three-story structure had been modeled after the estates of old, where the landed gentry lorded it over the peasants until the Irish War of Independence saw most of the lavish country estates leveled.

Pretentious upstart. Taking on airs. Lash snorted. He had as much contempt for Nolan as the man held for Lash. Other than a means to an end, neither man would have had anything to do with the other.

Lifting the brass dragon-head door knocker, he was surprised at its weight. Rather than tap it against the metal plate, he lifted it and let it fall. He found the resulting dull boom so satisfying that he did it three times more. He would have continued, but the door was snatched open, revealing a man dressed in a black suit, stiff white shirt, and bow tie.

With a sneer and a sweep of his arm, the butler indicated Lash should enter. The man's shiny patent leather shoes clicked sharply against the marble flooring as he led Lash through a sea of the gleaming stuff, passing several closed doors before stopping at the only one that stood open.

"Sir, your guest has arrived."

Duffy sat behind a massive mahogany desk, perusing a stack of documents. He didn't look up. Lash shifted irritably at the obvious slight.

Seconds passed before Duffy twitched his finger, and the butler stepped aside, allowing Lash to enter the book-lined room. The latch clicked as the door closed behind him.

He looked around for a chair and found two positioned in front of a small hearth.

"Don't bother. You're not staying." Duffy shuffled through the papers, pulling one from the stack before he looked up.

Lash wondered how the man kept his forked tongue from flicking between his lips. Narrowing his eyes, he would have liked nothing more than to reach over, grab the self-important git, drag him over his ridiculous desk, and show the snake who was the real predator in the room. Lash clenched his fists until they ached.

"You want to try it?" Duffy pulled a pistol he'd concealed under the desk and laid it atop the papers. Cocking an eyebrow, he waited for Lash to decide.

"One day, you'll get what's coming to you," Lash growled.

"That I will, but it won't be today," Duffy smirked. "And it won't be you I'll be answering to."

I wouldn't be so sure. Lash vowed.

"Wasn't it you who told me the McLoughlin's had that black dragon back in the air?" It wasn't really a question.

"Yeah, so?"

"What did I tell you to do about it?" Duffy picked at a hangnail.

"What's your point?" Lash growled. He only had so much patience for the pompous git.

Duffy jumped to his feet and slammed his fist against the dark wood. "Let me refresh your memory, Lash! Shoot Nocturne out of the sky. Does any part of that ring a bell, you pumped up thug?"

"Toby . . ."

"Don't. You don't get to blame this on that worthless kid of yours. He shot at my dragon, not McLoughlin's. And he didn't even hit the dragon. How big of a target does he need?"

"I . . ."

"I nothing!" Duffy shouted. "Do what you have to do. Cripple her, poison her, burn the barn down around her if that's what it takes. That dragon can't be allowed to fly competitively." Huffing, he sat down, picked up the gun, and turned it over in his hand before spearing Lash with a malevolent look. "Let me remind you, it's not just your life riding on this. There are people more dangerous than either you or me out there, and rest assured they won't forgive a two-time winner of the Labyrinth of Ruin showing up at the starting line." He raised the gun and pointed it at Lash's heart. "Get out."

Lash smoldered as he stared Duffy down. It took the sound of the gun cocking to make him reconsider his stand.

He took one step back, followed by another, his mind filled with rage. *We'll see who walks away in the end.* He vowed.

CHAPTER FIFTY

FLY NOCTURNE? JACKSON WHIPPED his head around. His da didn't look surprised at his wife's words. He just stared at the table, shaking his head.

"It's not going to happen, Lorelei." Cullum peered up through his brows and met Jackson's gaze.

"You don't get to make that decision alone, Cullum." Lorelei indicated all four of their boys seated around the table. "Last I checked, we're a family. We all contribute, and we all get a say. Especially when it comes to saving the farm."

Cullum leaned back in his chair. "Be reasonable, my love. Nocturne won't fly for any of us. Not even you."

He blames me. By making Nocturne my friend, I've ruined her and any chance to save the farm. Jackson's guilt hung like an anvil around his heart.

"Do you expect us to swallow that hogwash?" Lorelei moved around the table to take up a position behind Jackson's chair. "Our son rode Nocturne using ropes and twisty ties."

While Jackson should have found the warmth of his mum's hands on his shoulders comforting, he did not. That she was willing to stand against his da when his father was right, bothered him more than he thought possible.

"Don't remind me." Cullum dragged his hand over his jaw. "I still have nightmares. Flying Nocturne around the farm is bad enough, but to pit our son against the International Jockey community, the best riders in the world, and in the Labyrinth of Ruin of all races? It's not only ludicrous, it's total insanity. And you know it, Lorelei."

"No." Her hands tightened. "Admittedly, Jackson will need some training, but there's time before the race is upon us. I'll train him myself." Her fingers dug in.

Jackson winced. *She's afraid.*

"Count me in. I'll show this squirt the ropes." Robby flashed Jackson an exaggerated wink. "You didn't burn those ropes and twisty ties, did you, Da?"

"Not funny, Robby." Jackson squirmed at the memory of the day he'd been caught flying Nocturne.

"All questionable kidding aside." Aiden rolled his eyes at Robby. "I've felt Nocturne's feelings, and Da, that dragon is not going to be retrained. She's not the same dragon you worked with in the past. That race tore a hole in her heart." He paused to give Jackson a long look. "Jackson and Tivet filled that hole. She's theirs now. They're bonded so strongly that only death will break their connection." He rose and moved to stand with the others. "Nocturne's smart, experienced, and one of the smoothest riding dragons to ever take to the skies. She won't let anything happen to Jackson. I say, give them a chance."

"Mum is the best flight instructor in the world. How many times have I heard you say it?" Brandon pushed back his chair and joined Aiden and his mum. "I'm in. Let them fly."

Jackson, his heart in his throat, stared at his da as his gaze traveled over the family standing together in solidarity. The range of emotions that flickered over his features were fleeting, but one stood clear from the rest, and Jackson recognized it for what it was. He was terrified at the thought of Jackson riding Nocturne in the Labyrinth of Ruin. When Cullum turned to Jackson, he didn't look away. It was a test, and Jackson knew it as such. If he looked away now, showing even a hint of uncertainty, his da would say no, forfeiting their only chance to save the farm.

I have to try. Jackson attempted to calm his racing heart as he challenged the man he respected above all others.

"I can do this, Da." He reached up, covered his mum's hand, and looked at each of his brothers in turn before returning his gaze to his father's. "We can do this."

CHAPTER FIFTY-ONE

STOPPING IN FRONT OF NOCTURNE'S STALL, Jackson was greeted by a familiar sight: Tivet cuddled up between the black dragon's front legs. Glimmering black and shimmering white, no matter how many times he saw them together, Jackson still marveled at the contrast—the beauty.

Both dragons lifted their heads as he rolled the gate to the side.

~*What's wrong?* Tivet practically shouted his alarm.

"Why do you think there's something wrong?" Jackson answered, settling into the bedding. He didn't resist as Nocturne used her snout to gently roll him over onto his back. Tivet immediately snuffled Jackson's pockets.

"I don't have any tuna balls, you guys." Laughing, he pushed ineffectively at Nocturne's massive head.

~*Why not? We're hungry.* Tivet whined.

"Please, you had your dinner plus some of Nocturne's," Jackson said, sitting back up. "Da says you're going to get too fat to fly."

Tivet puffed a thin wisp of smoke and leaned against the larger dragon. ~*Never. You have no idea how much energy it takes to be as fast as me.*

"Are we a little high on ourselves?" Jackson smirked. "You making any progress on your fire? The smoke stream did seem a bit more substantial than last week."

~You didn't come here to talk about my fire. What's up? I'm tired. I need my sleep.

"Oh? Since I don't have any tuna balls, now you're sleepy?"

Nocturne curved her long neck around to include Jackson in their cuddle. He leaned back against the warmth of her scales and used his foot to nudge Tivet, who turned his colorful eyes on Jackson.

~And . . ?

"Alright. Da wants you to sleep in your enclosure."

~What? Why?

"There are several reasons, not the least of which is that you're old enough to have your own stall. You're not a baby anymore."

~This is about me eating Nocturne's food, right? I promise I'll stop.

"Yeah, right. That promise will only last until the next meal. Besides, that's not the reason."

~What is it then?

"Nocturne's going to fly in The Labyrinth of Ruin, and she'll need to be okay with you not being around every minute of every day."

~Isn't that the big race you guys are always going on about? The one in Europe?

"Yes."

~What's that got to do with me sleeping in a separate stall? Is it against the rules to have a companion for the flyers?

"Tivet, you won't be going."

~Not going? Why not. Tivet jumped to his feet, smoke

streaming from his snout. Nocturne raised her head in alarm, leaving Jackson to fall flat on his back.

"Don't ever let Da see you throwing a tantrum like that," Jackson said after he regained his seat.

~I would never hurt you. Tivet lowered his head between his legs, deflated.

"Da doesn't know that." Jackson patted the hay next to him. "Listen, you dunderhead, there's so much going on other than who sleeps where."

~Then tell me.

"We don't think it would be safe for you to be seen in Europe."

~Why?

"Well. . ." Jackson ran his fingers over Tivet's luminous scales. "Doc's been quietly doing research, and he thinks that you might be the last of a species thought to be extinct for centuries."

~It would hardly take a genius to figure that out, now would it? Tivet snarked, ruffling his wings.

"Don't be disrespectful. Doc cares about you as much as the rest of the family. But he's afraid the authorities might try to take you away from us if word gets out."

~Take me where? Tivet began to tremble. *~Can they do that?*

Nocturne's head rose, and a deep rumble shook her body as she looked around for what frightened Tivet.

"You need to relax before Nocturne burns the barn down. Besides, Da would never let them take you."

~I'm sorry.

"You haven't done anything wrong. It's just that things will get complicated around here, and you need to be on your best behavior."

~How come they suddenly want to fly Nocturne? Your da must know that she won't fly for anybody but you.

"Yeah, that's sorta the problem." His features twisted. "Arguably the biggest one."

~That's for sure.

"If we don't find a way to get the tax money, we'll lose the farm."

~Lose the farm?

"You've known that things have been tight since Duffy stole our best-paying client?" Jackson didn't wait for a response. "And now . . . well, now they're dire. The land tax will be due soon, and we won't have enough money to cover it."

~So, you're going to fly Nocturne?

"Yes." Jackson sifted his fingers through the bedding. "I don't have a choice."

~You can do it.

"Flying in a straight line is one thing, Tivet. This race isn't about flying from point A to point B. It's designed to test speed, maneuverability, and, most of all, endurance. Only the best of the best, rider and dragon, can hope to finish this race, let alone win. I'm just a creature deaf kid who's never flown a race."

~How long do we have?

CHAPTER FIFTY-TWO

JACKSON TAPPED HIS RIGHT HEEL three times, and Nocturne responded by banking left to start a slow, downward spiral in preparation for a precision landing. Their objective was a circle of whitewashed stones on the grass a thousand feet beneath them.

~Looking good for a bullseye landing.

~Don't lead us in Tivet. We have to do this on our own. Jackson wouldn't get an accurate gauge on the circle until they'd lost more altitude. Over the weeks of training, his mum had continued to decrease the circle's size until it barely contained Nocturne, and only if she curled her tail to the side as she touched down. However, Jackson quickly learned that Nocturne could see things far better than he could from this height. Once signaled, he needed to trust her to land within the circle's confines. Trust was one thing Jackson understood. But complete trust was another hurdle he'd yet to overcome.

"So many signals," he muttered as he tried to remember if he'd given Nocturne three taps or four. He and Tivet had devised the signals so that he could communicate with Nocturne when Tivet wasn't around.

"Pay attention, Jackson," his mum's voice in his earpiece got him back in the game. "Relax, remember you're not a monkey clinging to her back. You're a partner in this maneuver."

How does she know I'm puckered up like a pair of lips sucking on a lemon? He tried to relax without losing his seat. But astride a massive being with a mind of its own while hundreds of feet in the air, called for a level of fluidity he wasn't sure he'd managed as yet. It was the hardest thing he'd had to overcome during their weeks of training in the Mountains of the Boar's Pass and the Twelve Bens.

With the ocean a short flight east and Lough Inagh and the sharp-peaked quartzite summits and ridges of the Twelve Bens to the west of their campsite, this was the closest they could come to replicating the type of conditions they would face in the Labyrinth of Ruin.

His mum made good use of all the area's assets, with only one day a week for rest; the pace had proven exhausting. Even rain and gale-force winds were no excuse to ground them. The Labyrinth of Ruin would not be suspended due to unfavorable weather conditions.

"Just another challenge to overcome," his mum's favorite adage.

"Jackson, pay attention, you're drifting and likely to land in the Lough." His mum's tone harshened.

Today, they practiced in the Inagh Valley, where there was enough room to lay out the stone circle.

"Pick it up, Jackson," Lorelei snapped. "Did you forget? This is a time trial. If you want to win, you can't take twenty minutes to land."

~Argh! This is my least favorite part. Jackson tapped two times on Nocturne's left side. She pulled her wings from full spread to half furled, and the leisurely circling turned into a gut-wrenching drop. Arrowing for the ground, the white

bullseye grew larger at an alarming rate.

Tivet rocketed past, his wings close to his body, and whooped. *~What do you mean? This is the best part.*

Crouched low over Nocturne's withers, Jackson's thighs pressed painfully against the swell of the saddle's pommel. He peered through his goggles at the fast-approaching ground and the puffs of white that scattered in every direction as the long-tailed sheep who populated the area sprinted for safety. He braced for Nocturne's wings to expand fully and he tapped both heels simultaneously. Jackson's chest compressed with the force of the deceleration, squeezing out the last breath he'd taken.

Nocturne back-winged, and within seconds, they settled well within the circle's confines.

"Good job." Lorelei jogged over to rub Nocturne's nostril as she praised the dragon. "My sweet, you're taking such good care of my baby."

"Mum," Jackson whined, embarrassed.

"You'll always be my lamb." Lorelei smiled at him. "Your landings are perfect. Now, you have to work on speed. Starting the dive earlier will help save time. Try again."

"Again?" Jackson had yet to catch his breath fully, and he was tired. Though if asked, he'd be forced to admit he was getting stronger and fitter with each day's passing. He frowned down at his mum and opened his mouth to speak. She raised her hand, stopping him.

"The nomination money's spent, and we're running short on time. You can sleep for a month after the race ends, and the two of you have won the prize. We're trying to teach you in a matter of weeks what normally takes a decade to learn. You have the best dragon, Jackson. Now, mo chróí, we must make you the best rider for her. When decades become days, we have none to spare. So, again."

Jackson waited for his mother to clear the circle before he

fisted the martingale on Nocturne's neck, leaned forward, thighs clenched, and yelled. "Away."

~*Whoo-hoo*. Tivet shrieked in Jackson's head.

The sun sparked against the big dragon's scales, highlighting the depth of their blue-black sheen. The iridescent streak of light that was Tivet circled them twice as Nocturne rocketed from the ground.

~*Show off*. Jackson couldn't help but laugh even as he held firm against the g-force that threatened to tear him from the saddle.

LEITIR BHRIOCÁIN, AS PART of the Maamturk range, enjoyed a sharp, v-shaped pass with weathered quartzite peaks and was today's destination. Jackson, though physically and mentally exhausted from the non-stop training of the past weeks, was excited about the trial that lay ahead.

He glanced at Robby, who was riding the lead dragon his mum usually rode. Tivet, the ornery little squirt, was showing little regard for safe distance protocols and zipping all over the place. While the dragons he and Robby rode had gotten used to Tivet's antics, Robby kept ducking in alarm when Tivet came too close. Jackson laughed as his brother flinched for the umpteenth time.

"Are you kidding me?" Robby's frustration sounded through Jackson's earbud. "How do you put up with this?"

"Tivet's been invaluable for Jackson's training," Lorelei answered for Jackson through their open channel. "It's going to get much tighter than that in the heat of the race."

Callum and Robby had arrived at the training camp the previous night. They carried fresh feed for the dragons and news about the weather. And it wasn't good. They would have to push up their timeline; a series of massive storms were rolling in off the Atlantic, and they would need to get out ahead of the bad weather. Today would be the final day of training. So he and Robby were flying a training pass through the Leitir Bhriocáin.

Short of driving Nocturne into the ground or a cliff face, Robby's job was to badger her and Jackson at every opportunity, replicating race conditions as closely as possible to what they would be experiencing on the final day of the Labyrinth of Ruin. Dragon racing wasn't for the tentative.

While Nocturne might arguably be the fastest dragon that had ever flown, she couldn't fly full-out the whole way in a race of that distance. She might avoid larger dragons and overzealous jockeys that way, but she'd have nothing to give at the end of the race, where the win lay. Today's training was designed to provide Jackson with a taste of close-quarters flying coupled with aggressive challenges.

He smiled to himself. What nobody knew, including his mum, was how whenever he and Nocturne were out of her sight, behind a mountain, a cloud, or a fog bank, he'd been letting her attempt to replicate Tivet's insane moves. And while she would never fly as fast or be able to outmaneuver Tivet, Nocturne was no longer like any other dragon Jackson had ever seen. She was a graceful ballerina who danced on wings rather than pink pointe shoes.

~*Tivet,* Jackson mindspoke as they neared the beginning of the course Lorelei had laid out. ~*Da doesn't want you to interfere. Robby is going to challenge me and Nocturne. Okay? They'll be watching from the ridge. You should join them.*

~*Robby'll never get close enough to give you a hard time. Nocturne is going to smoke him.*

~*She may, but it won't be because I leave him in our wake. They want to see how I handle pressure. This is my last chance to prove myself. I don't want Mum to have any excuse to ground us.*

~She won't. I've done a superb job training both of you. Jackson could well imagine the smug smile behind Tivet's words. *If he could smile, that is.*

~Yes, you have.

As he and Robby flew to the beginning of the course, Jackson felt more confident than he'd felt since the challenging weeks of training had begun.

~Do me proud.

The wind tore away Jackson's laugh as the black dragon's powerful wings pushed through the air to gain altitude before topping the quartzite peak and diving into the v-shaped pass on the other side.

⬖⬖⬖⬖

EXHAUSTED, JACKSON SAT BEFORE the campfire. Though he'd tried, he couldn't wipe the smile from his face.

"I've never seen anything like it." Robby pushed his hair off his forehead, the action was turning into a nervous habit. "Those boys aren't going to know what hit them. Tell me again how you taught Nocturne to do . . . what did you call them? Belly-rolls?"

"I didn't teach her, Tivet did. Why are you having so much trouble believing that?"

"That little squirt is the fastest, most maneuverable dragon I've had the good fortune to come across." Cullum laughed. Jackson couldn't help but remember the day he'd brought Tivet home when his da had said he couldn't keep him. And now the orphan might be responsible for saving the farm.

"I'm glad you're all so tickled." Lorelei joined them at the fire and settled next to Cullum. "But have you considered how dangerous those maneuvers were? My heart was in my throat the whole time."

"Dragon racing is dangerous." Cullum shrugged. "As long as the rider knows what he's doing, and the harness doesn't break . . ." He looked up. "Besides, that boy knows how to ride. He's got the makings of the best apprentice I've seen take to the saddle. You did a good job, Lorelei. But then, I would expect nothing less." Cullum reached over and tugged her closer. "I love you, mo chrói."

"Ugh, don't start that stuff." Robby groaned. "So, do I need to ask? Does Jackson get the go-ahead?"

Lorelei looked over at Jackson, her eyes narrowed, and he held his breath.

"We'll leave in the morning." Lorelei grinned. "We have a race to win."

CHAPTER FIFTY-THREE

IT HAD BEEN GOOD TO BE HOME, even for such a short time. While Jackson enjoyed camping in the Inagh Valley, there was nothing like a hot shower and his warm bed.

"Doc, the ship is scheduled to dock tonight at Cherbourg. Your cousin, Jules, has assured me he has everything ready." Cullum glanced up from the map spread across the kitchen table.

"Yes. Jules will be picking them up at the dock and taking them to his farm," Doc confirmed.

Lorelei and Jackson's brothers had taken a ship from Dublin to France the day before. They carried with them the gear the race team would need for an extended stay in France. With genuine threats on Nocturne's life, shipping her by boat had been out of the question. Leaving only one alternative— flying out of Ireland in the dark of night.

"And you're sure that he's arranged for feed for the entirety of our stay?"

Tiring of the conversation, Jackson angled toward the hearth. Though the fire had burned down, the remaining coal emitted plenty of warmth, and Jackson intended to enjoy that warmth while he still could. He and his da were leaving at nightfall to beat the bad weather that loomed ever larger off the north-western coast. While the storm, the first of several, was taking a more northerly route, it was coming far faster than anticipated, and the forecast called for it to last for days.

By leaving the mainland at Belfast, crossing the Irish Sea to Blackpool before angling down and passing over the British midlands, skirting London, and on to Dover on the east coast, they hoped to miss the full brunt of the storm.

The most dangerous leg of their journey would be over the Irish Sea. Flying over open water in frigid conditions would be hazardous. His da had pointed out the Isle of Man on the map, which was midway through the crossing. Assuring Jackson that this was the safest, if not the shortest, route to Great Britain in case they were forced into landing.

"I've made him aware of the threats we could be facing. Feed being the most critical." Doc paused to stir more sugar into his mug. "Jules and his associates are anxious to help. The level of criminality on their circuit has risen to the point it's being discussed openly. Supposedly, the racing federation is investigating each allegation in partnership with French intelligence. But they're not making a lot of headway. Finding someone to testify against the mob is difficult, if not impossible, as you can imagine."

"That would be an understatement. Is Jules still confident each farm we land at will be safe?"

"He is. That doesn't mean we should let our guard down." Doc sighed. "As much as I hate to agree with you, changing farms each night is the smart thing to do until we are forced to stable in the official quarantine barns."

"And that's where the bad guys will pull out all the stops. You still think they'll use a shakedown ruse to plant something disqualifying on us?"

"Jules said we could count on it." Doc nodded. "Did you

get Paddy O'Bryan to agree to make the trip?"

Jackson knew Paddy, a stocky guy with a prodigious paunch. It was hard to believe he'd ever flown in a race, let alone been one of the best jockeys of his generation. More importantly, Paddy had been the steward who oversaw Jackson as he flew a training race to qualify for his journeyman's license. He'd even given Jackson some pointers on his seat.

"He was thrilled." Cullum smiled. "Paddy will go to war to keep corruption from infecting Irish Racing."

"Well, it's settled then. Jules has a vet he trusts until I can join you in Chantilly when the pre-race festival begins."

Cullum looked over at the other person at the table who had maintained his silence throughout the discussion. "How about you, Shamus? Are you and your brothers ready to keep both your farm and mine going in our absence? I know it's asking a lot."

"Every person in the village, not just the dragon trainers, has already stepped up to help. We have patrols watching Duffy and the travelers camping on his land. They can't pick their noses without one of us knowing about it. The only thing you have to worry about is winning that race." Shamus turned his gaze on Jackson. "The entire village is rooting for you, Jack."

Oh boy. Shamus's words struck Jackson hard. If he failed, not only was his family's farm at stake but also an entire way of life for many others.

With this revelation weighing him down, he left the warm kitchen and headed out to spend the next few hours with Tivet.

CHAPTER FIFTY-FOUR

IF ASKED, JACKSON COULDN'T HAVE said which had been more brutal, saying goodbye to Tivet or the two-hour flight over the Irish Sea. Pushed along the storm's leading edge, the tailwind shortened the time he and his father spent over the open water. However, that same wind and moisture-laden air made the night flight harsh.

Once the lights of Belfast faded behind them, what had been scattered cloud cover thickened. Then abruptly, their only light source, the moon and stars, disappeared.

"Da?" Jackson spoke into his headpiece, his tone laced with panic. Set adrift in a lightless void, unable to tell up from down, claustrophobia sank its claws deep. For all he knew, Nocturne could be flying them straight into the storm-roiled sea.

"Jackson," his da's voice responded, calm and measured.

"Da. I can't see." The feel of the cold wind on his skin, how his body no longer reacted in concert with Nocturne's familiar movements, amped up his terror to the point he thought his heart would explode from his chest.

"You don't need to, son. Trust your dragon. Nocturne won't fly into the water. What do dragons and owls have in common? Can you tell me?"

Jackson clung to his father's words.

"Jackson?"

"Night vision."

"That's right. Look to your left. Do you see my night flight beacon? Now, reach up and flip the switch I showed you on your helmet." A small light shone off to Jackson's left as his da urged the brown dragon he rode to overtake Nocturne. "You remember where it is?"

"Yes," Jackson responded. His breath came easier as the panic began to ease. He flicked the switch. Its soft glow didn't reach far, but it was enough to orient himself in the space he occupied.

"I'm sorry, Da."

"Don't be. It's me that owes *you* an apology. What with everything else that's been going on, I didn't think to check whether you and your mum had done any night-flight training. You didn't panic, and I'm proud of you."

With adrenaline still fueling the tremors that shook him from head to toe, Jackson wasn't sure he would agree with his da's assessment. Leaning over, he spread his arms over Nocturne's sleek scales. "I promise I'll never doubt you again."

With the wind whipping his words away, he was surprised when Nocturne bobbed her head, seemingly in response.

THE HOURS DRAGGED BY, FORCING Jackson to concentrate on staying awake. Cullum indicated points of interest as they passed over the British countryside, which helped. But Jackson still found himself nodding off and was jerked awake when his da's voice rang in his ear.

"Look down, Jackson, the White Cliffs of Dover. That's a sight to remember."

His fatigue forgotten, Jackson stared in wonder at the gleaming white cliffs that fell away to the multi-hued water of the Straights of Dover. He'd seen pictures of the cliffs, but nothing could do them justice. You had to see them for yourself.

They angled their mounts to get a closer view of the sheer chalk surface streaked with black flint. He glanced seaward at the massive container ships lined up to the far horizon as they sailed through the narrow straight. Jackson marveled at the tiny figures on the vessel who excitedly pointed and waved. He could only imagine how excited those watchers were to see two giant dragons sweep across the massive cliff face.

Jackson whooped with glee, waving back as he and Nocturne swooped low over the ocean-going craft.

Nearing the French coast and their destination, much of his body felt numb. With only two stops at English dragon farms to feed and water their dragons, Jackson had thought he'd known what tired felt like while training with his mum. Since he had found very little in the way of sleep before they left, his mind had grown fuzzy, his muscles sluggish and were slow to respond as the hours ground on. At some point, Jackson recognized he was less a dragon rider than merely a piece of baggage, subject to the whim of the dragon he rode.

He laughed to himself as he realized, more than anything, how he missed Tivet's constant chatter—his joyful buzz-bombing. *That would have kept me alert.*

"Good thing Nocturne doesn't need guidance," Jackson confided to his father through his headpiece.

"We're almost there. Look to the left. Do you see that slope with all the grapevines? There are open fields beyond that point, and that's where we're headed."

"We're almost there, Nocturne." In preparation, Jackson adjusted his seat and hoped his legs would hold him on dismount. His brothers would never let him hear the end of it if he landed face-first in the thick grass he could see from the air.

Once they'd flown close enough, Jackson spotted at least seven tiny figures rushing from a huge barn large enough to house more dragons than he'd ever seen in one place before. His excitement began to nibble away at his fatigue.

And there wasn't just one barn; there were four of similar size. *How big is this place?*

He spotted a triangle of large white circles drawn in the open field and tapped the code for landing on Nocturne's shoulder. Jackson circled while Cullum landed his dragon. Once the pair were safely on the ground, Jackson decided to show off a little and directed Nocturne to a dead-center landing in the smallest circle of the three.

On the ground, Nocturne flared her wings, arched her neck, and trumpeted her arrival. Answering calls from the barn's occupants filled the air.

"Yeah, yeah, you're definitely all that. Aren't you?" His safety straps released, Jackson prepared to dismount and eyed the ground. Before he could commit, Nocturne lowered her bulk, making it much less likely he'd faceplant if his rubbery legs failed to hold him. "You're a lifesaver."

On the ground, Jackson leaned against Nocturne's warmth, grateful for her support. She turned her head, looking for praise. Grinning, he rubbed her eye ridge.

"I owe you one," He whispered into her ear slot, surprised when she nodded and nudged his chest. *Did she understand what I said?* Jackson reeled at the thought. *Nah, she's only responding to my voice.*

CHAPTER FIFTY-FIVE

THE AIR IN HIS STALL WAS COLD, and Tivet liked it that way. He was hungry, and Shamus was late again. Rolling onto his back, he spread his wings across the bedding. Wiggling his legs, he entertained himself by studying the differences between his front and back appendages.

Jackson had spent quite a bit of time explaining why the dissimilarities existed. How, just like lizards, Tivet had hands and feet. And humans, too, Tivet thought. Extending and retracting his slightly rounded claws, he marveled at how much they had grown since he'd been rescued. Moving his gaze to his back feet, he stretched the much longer toes with their razor-sharp, non-retractable talons. Jackson had postulated that the hands and claws were for grabbing and holding, while the much longer and sharper talons on Tivet's back feet eviscerated the prey.

"For slicing and dicing," Jackson had pointed out. At the memory, Tivet considered that perhaps Jackson wasn't as much of a pacifist as he'd initially appeared. He was certainly more assertive than when he first stormed into the Travellers' camp, maybe even aggressive. It didn't matter. Tivet admired

every aspect of Jackson's persona.

The slap of leather-soled boots sounded in the breezeway, interrupting Tivet's thoughts. *Shamus.*

Tivet considered getting up and decided against it. His tummy might have told him he was hungry, but his mind said otherwise. The truth was he missed Jackson and Nocturne so much it hurt.

That he was forced to stay in his stall was his fault; he knew it, but it wouldn't change how he felt. Allowing Shamus to outfit him with a halter and rope, then leading Tivet around on the end of what was a leash wasn't happening. When he'd allowed it with Jackson, they both knew it was just for show. And, since Cullum relented, the halter and lead shank were a thing of the past.

"How are you doing? You wee beasty?"

It was the same question every time. Tivet didn't respond; he just continued to lie on his back and ignore the man.

"Why are you on your back? Does your tummy hurt?" Shamus rolled back the door and looked in the feed tub, where the stale feed was less than half gone. After he'd checked the water, he approached.

"Let's have a look." He reached toward Tivet's tummy, only to snatch his hand back when he hissed. "Now that's no way to behave." Shamus's sunny demeanor shifted slightly, but Tivet could sense the man's mood. It wasn't aggressive like Lash or Toby's would have been. Still, he'd made Shamus uneasy, and Tivet almost felt bad, almost.

Turning his head away, he listened as the man left the stall, closing the door behind him. Shamus didn't go far. A dial tone alerted Tivet that the man was making use of the phone that hung on the wall one stall down. Tivet got to his feet and moved closer to listen through the bars at what the man was saying. He hoped that Shamus wasn't calling a vet.

"May I speak with Cullum, please?"

Even with his superior hearing, Tivet found himself straining to listen to both sides of the conversation.

"Shamus, is something wrong?"

"Oh, hi Cullum, not really. It's just that little white dragon is lying flat on his back and hisses at me when I try to get close." Tivet could hear the concern in Shamus's voice, which might have bothered him a little, after all, if he hadn't been so out of sorts with the whole situation. "It's just that he's such an odd little thing. I can't seem to get on his good side. I'm worried that he might be colicky, is all."

Little, I'll show him little.

"Is he eating?"

"Yes, but not as much as he should, and I can't get him to accept the halter, so he hasn't come out of his stall since you left."

"Is he on his back with his feet stuck in the air and his wings spread?"

"Yes to both."

"He's pouting." Tivet could hear Cullum snicker.

"Pouting? Dragons pout? I can't say I've heard of that before, but then he's no ordinary dragon, is he? Alright, you know your dragons, I'll hold off calling the vet."

"How's everything else, Shamus?"

"Some of the guys have seen Lash's kid sneaking around off and on, but he stuck to the main road, so there wasn't anything we could do about it. With our twenty-four-hour patrols, he couldn't have gotten close enough to the barns to do any harm. The boy has mostly been sticking close to the Travellers' camp over at Duffy's place. And neither Duffy nor Lash have been seen since right after you left. Are you having any problems over there?"

"Not yet. We've managed to stay one step ahead of any trouble pointed in our direction. We changed farms every day until we were forced, by the rules, to move into the official stabling reserved for contestants. With the race beginning the day after tomorrow, Jackson won't leave Nocturne's side unless one of the family is in the stall with her. Association guards have been assigned to all the contestants. They're posted outside each stall, which isn't good enough for us. We're all taking shifts to protect Jack and Nocturne. Maybe from guards, racing officials . . . who knows. Two dragons have already been pulled from the feature race under suspicious circumstances. Racing officials are staying pretty tight-lipped about what exactly happened to them."

"Wow. I know you expected this, but still, the pressure must be awful. How are Jackson and Nocturne handling it?"

"You know, Nocturne, Shamus. She's a pro, and now that she's recovered, as long as Jackson's with her, I think we have to be more concerned with her flaming anyone who gets too close to Jackson. She's gotten pretty broody over both him and Tivet." Callum lowered his voice, and Tivet barely caught the words that followed.

"As for Jackson, he's quaking in his boots. He tries to hide it, but with the stakes being what they are, he's terrified of failing the family. Truthfully, Shamus, I wish I'd let that quirky little dragonet come along. He's got more confidence than any dragon I've ever seen, and it influences Jack in such a positive way. Those two together are something special. Throw Nocturne into the mix, and they make quite the triumvirate. I wouldn't bet against them, that's for sure."

"You might be right," Shamus agreed. "It's not like word won't spread eventually about Tivet. He's too unusual."

"Hang on, Shamus, this phone is right outside Nocturne's stall." Tivet heard Cullum shout. "Hey, Jack, come here for a second. Let's see if the sound of Jackson's voice can influence that ornery little git."

"Is Tivet going to be able to hear him?"

"Trust me, that dragonet can hear a piece of bacon hitting

the frying pan in our kitchen from his stall." Cullum laughed.

"What's up? Is Tivet all right?" Tivet's heart swelled at the beloved voice.

"Yes, it's Shamus, and your wee beasty has been giving him a bad time. Speak to him. Maybe if he hears your voice, he'll behave."

Shamus smiled when he turned to see Tivet with his snout poking through the bars of the stall gate.

"Tivet?" Jackson shouted over the phone. "You have no idea how much Nocturne and I wish you were here. It would make us both sad to know that you're unhappy. Please, Tivet, Shamus is doing us a huge favor by watching over the farm. Can you do this for me and Nocturne? We miss you to bits. Oh, and don't waste food. I've got a pretty good idea what you're doing."

Tivet chuffed loudly.

"Whatever, mate," Jackson laughed and rang off.

Later that night, when Shamus made his rounds, he found Tivet's feed tub wedged against the stall door, polished to a shine, without a speck of food stuck to the bottom or sides.

"Well, I'll be. You'd think the little tyke could understand English," Shamus said as he opened the stall door to remove the tub. "Wouldn't that be something?"

Yes. Yes, it would. Tivet rolled onto his back and closed his eyes. Sleep came quickly.

CHAPTER FIFTY-SIX

FAVORING HER RIGHT SIDE, SARAH CREPT through the parked caravans. By sticking close to the shadows, she hoped to make it to her grandmother's caravan, where she knew she'd be safe—a place where Toby wouldn't dare torture her.

Stumbling over something she didn't bother to identify, she clutched her aching ribs, gasping for air—every day since her half-brother had been accused of shooting the dragon rider, Toby would get Sarah alone. Calling her a traitor, he'd punch her where the bruises wouldn't show, and he wouldn't stop until she groveled at his feet. But last night's beating was the worst yet, and she was pretty sure as she lay on the ground, the boot to her side fractured a rib.

Peering around the last colorful caravan before her grandmother's, there was no sign of Toby, and she sighed with relief.

"Where do you think you're going, Traitor?" Toby's hate-filled voice sounded right behind her. "We haven't had our talk today."

Sarah didn't quite manage to swallow her scream as Toby yanked her into the shadows.

"You in pain, Freak?" Toby pushed her up against the caravan's wheel, raised his hand, hesitated, then jammed his fingers in her ribs instead.

Grunting in pain, Sarah doubled over, unable to utter a sound. Not that she would have if she could. Toby had warned her what he would do to her if she ever snitched on him again. He said they'd never find Sarah's body once he dumped it in the peat bogs. She had no reason to doubt him. Toby might not be as bad as their father, but he was well on his way.

"How about I kick the other side?" Sarah could see a flash of white as he grinned in anticipation. "Even you up?"

"Here. What's going on?" Sarah sank to her knees at the sound of their grandmother's voice.

"Nothing." Toby stepped back. "Sarah fell. I was going to help her up." Toby was as prolific a liar as Lash. But then why wouldn't he be? He'd learned from the best. Sarah figured they were good at it, not because they practiced but because they felt entitled to their own truths.

"Listen here, you hooligan." Fawnie's voice drew closer. "Your da isn't here, which means I'm clan leader until he returns. And if I find you abusing your sister again, it'll be you getting a whipping before the clan fire. Do you understand me?"

"This freak is not my sister." Toby blustered and pointed an accusing finger. "She's a traitor to our clan."

"Shut your gob," Fawnie said, shaking her fist in Toby's face. "Until my son returns, I'm the law. If you want to test me, go right ahead. Let's see who has the most pull around here."

With her hands firmly on her hips, Fawnie leaned right in. But from the look on his face, Sarah wasn't sure Toby was going to back down.

His hands balled into fists at his sides. The boy was bigger than his grandmother and he continued to challenge her for several heartbeats. Sarah began to wonder if he would. Finally, he turned away with a huff, but not before he shot Sarah a baleful look. She knew that look and what it promised. There was more pain in store for her—plenty more.

CHAPTER FIFTY-SEVEN

RACE DAY WAS HERE, AND Jackson's stomach felt squeezy at the thought. Nocturne, lying on her side, opened an eye as he entered the stall and took a seat beside her.

"Listen, don't be afraid. Yesterday, an anonymous letter was delivered. When Mum opened it, she found a warning saying if we didn't go back to where we came from, we'd face the consequences. What do you think, Nocturne?" He stroked the soft scales around her nostrils, not expecting a response, but he needed to talk. "Do you think Da will scratch us from the race?"

Nocturne curved her long neck around Jackson, pulling him in for a cuddle. "I know you won't let anything happen to me. But Da says nothing in this world is worth risking an injury to either of us. Or worse." His voice trailed off.

Nocturne raised up, and wisps of smoke streamed from her nostrils.

Jackson clamored to his feet.

"You understand me?" A majestic movement of her head was answer enough. So, it was true, Nocturne had learned the human language. "Did Tivet teach you?"

Her response was a slight twitch of her shoulders. Tivet may not have set out to teach Nocturne, but in him learning to speak dragon, Nocturne had learned the English language.

"Oh my gosh!" Why hadn't he figured it out sooner? But Jackson knew it now and he wouldn't let that knowledge go to waste. Spreading his arms across Nocturne's massive chest, he felt heat building.

"It's me that he doesn't have faith in. Not you."

"Well, you're wrong." Jackson turned as his father arrived. "And if you don't hurry, you'll be late to the jockey's quarters."

Jackson threw himself into his father's arms. "I love you, Da."

"And I love you." Cullum tightened his hold. "Did I hear you talking to Nocturne? You think she understands your words?" He chuckled, ruffling Jackson's ginger curls as he released his grip. "I don't know about words, but she can sense feelings. So, it might be wise to go over there and reassure her."

"Da," Jackson lowered his voice and glanced into the shed row. "Tivet taught Nocturne to understand everything we say."

"Jackson, we don't have time for this." Cullum frowned. "We have to hurry."

"I'm not joking. Tivet talks to me in my head. The dragons have a language of their own. Since Tivet wasn't raised with other dragons, he had to learn it from Nocturne. And I just figured it out. While he was learning dragon, Nocturne was learning English."

"You hear Tivet and now Nocturne talking in your head?" Cullum looked skeptical. "That's not possible."

"Not Nocturne, only Tivet. But she understands our words. Isn't this way better than communicating through impressions and feelings, like dragon speakers? Plus, I'll still have the physical signals to fall back on when she can't hear me."

"Da, they're announcing the last call for all riders to the jock's room." Brandon waited outside the stall.

"Tonight, you and I will have a long talk about keeping secrets." The look Cullum gave Jackson left little doubt how that conversation would go.

⁂

DRESSED IN THE FAMILY RACING COLORS, Jackson took the saddle from Aiden and waited for the Clerk of Scales to note the weight on his clipboard.

Stepping off the scales, he handed the equipment back to his brother. Aiden had taken out a valet license with the racing board soon after their arrival in France. And as Jackson's valet, Aiden would be the only person, other than Jackson and Cullum, authorized to touch Nocturne's tack. They weren't willing to take a chance with a girth strap, stirrup leather, or any part of the equipment being tampered with.

When Jackson and Cullum arrived at the boxlike building at the far end of the grandstand near the saddling area, Aiden had been waiting for them with their equipment held protectively in his arms, and there it would stay until he placed it on Nocturne's back.

Though plain on the outside, the interior of the building was colorful, mainly due to the dozens of racing silks that hung from hooks on the ceiling.

Standing before an open-fronted locker, one of many along the building's back wall, Jackson was taking deep breaths, trying to settle his nerves. Since he'd arrived in the room, Harris was the only jockey who had done anything other than stare—and only briefly in passing before moving on to a locker several spaces down the row.

Refolding his street clothes for the umpteenth time, Jackson felt someone step up behind him. Turning, he was surprised to see three riders, already dressed in their racing silks, closing ranks around him. If their body language was any gauge, they didn't look like they were there to wish him luck.

Jackson raised his chin and crossed his arms over his chest. He didn't say anything. He didn't need to. *They won't shiv me right here in front of everybody.* Jackson quirked an eyebrow.

"Four grand, and you don't finish in the money." The man standing directly in front of Jackson said. He'd been pointed out to Jackson as the guy who rode exclusively for people associated with the mob. Tall and slender, the man had a don't-mess-with-me vibe about him.

"Is that a question?" Jackson wasn't sure what he was expecting, but this sure wasn't it. Talk about brazen.

"No." A second man spoke, shorter and more muscular than the first—the look on his face was no friendlier than the first.

"Make it easy on yourself," The last guy added. "Take the money, rookie . . ." He flicked his hand. "Or not. So that you understand, you won't be finishing the race either way. We'll make sure of it."

Jackson was dumbfounded at their blatant disregard for the law. And right out in the open.

"Don't be stupid." When Jackson failed to reply, the leader added. "Take the money, and we'll leave you alone."

Jackson did the only thing he could think to do: he turned his back and refolded his shirt for the umpteenth time.

"Fine, you've been warned." The three men walked away, talking amongst themselves.

Jackson dropped onto the bench in front of his locker. He no longer felt up to the task of standing.

"What was that all about?" Aiden approached, a tight grip on the armful of tack.

Jackson leaned over his spread knees. He felt like he was going to be sick.

"Hey, kid, talk to me." Aiden dumped the tack at their feet and sat down next to him.

Jackson carefully looked around before answering. He kept his voice down. "They offered me four thousand to not finish in the money."

Aiden's face clouded over; his lips stretched into a thin line. "Is that so? Well, let's see how the stewards feel about that." Aiden started to rise.

"No!" His voice firm, Jackson laid a hand on Aiden's thigh. "Don't. We can't prove it, and there's no time anyway. Besides, they'll never get close enough to Nocturne to do us any harm."

"You're right. At least for today," Aiden sighed. "You'll be safe in the gymkhana event. But they'll try something tonight, tomorrow, or the next day."

"Trust me, Aiden, we'll be okay. They'll be so far behind, they won't just be staring at our hind end, they'll be wondering where we went."

"Yeah, you should smoke them in the Labyrinth of Ruin," Aiden whispered ominously. "But that's where they hit Nocturne before and where they're sure to try again if, whoever's behind this doesn't find a way to eliminate her over the next two days."

A cloud of butterflies took flight in Jackson's stomach as the call came for the valets. "I guess we'll just have to be extra vigilant."

"Right, like we haven't been? Da will know what to do."

"Exactly." Jackson winked as Aiden gathered the equipment. "We got this, big brother."

CHAPTER FIFTY-EIGHT

CULLUM TRIED TO CALM NOCTURNE through their connection. The excited dragon was on her toes, prancing around on the end of the shank, and she wasn't in a listening mood.

"Steady, you know the drill, pretty girl. Jackson won't be here until you're wearing the tack. So, let's get this done." He glanced around before lowering his voice. "I know that you understand me. Jackson told me."

Nocturne lowered her head until Cullum stared into one large glimmering eye. She blinked, then peeled her lips far enough back to reveal razor-sharp teeth.

"What the heck?" Aiden set the tack on the ground, prepared to help. "Is she threatening you?"

"Not at all." Cullum laughed. "That dragon is letting me know she's gotten one over on me. Isn't that right, Queen Bee?"

Nocturne relaxed long enough for Aiden to set the saddle, then reared onto her hind legs, wings spread, and roared a challenge into the sky.

"She's . . ." Aiden raised his hands. "I've never seen her act like this. You'd think she'd never raced before."

"On the muscle and ready to fly." Cullum grinned as he waited for her to get it out of her system. "All right, big girl, here comes Jackson. I'm counting on you to take care of my son today."

Nocturne stilled, leaning in, and Cullum rested a hand on her broad forehead. Their connection felt solemn, like a sacred oath. "Thank you."

"Hey, what's going on?" Jackson bounded up. "Is Nocturne okay?"

"She's fine. We were sharing a moment." Cullum gave her one more pat before he turned to Jackson. "You've memorized the course. It's timed, so you don't have to be too precise as long as you stay within the boundaries. Nocturne's a pro at this, so you shouldn't have anything to worry about. However, a time advantage going into the next two rounds wouldn't hurt. Remember that style points carry a bigger weight than time. So don't try to get fancy by shaving the sticks."

"No worries," Jackson said. He took two quick steps and used Nocturne's front leg to vault into the saddle.

"Well, that was impressive." Cullum exchanged a surprised look with Aiden. "Can you do that?"

Aiden laughed, shaking his head as he watched Jackson strap in before urging Nocturne toward the starting line. "Lil bro's been practicing."

AS THEY APPROACHED THE STARTING line, Jackson was surprised at how quickly the soft breeze from earlier in the day had turned blustery. Blowing from the south, this had to be the leading edge of the next in the series of storms reportedly stacking up in the Atlantic. Forecasted to hit the mainland further north, Jackson had figured, sooner or later, they would have to face at least one of these storm fronts. He just wished it hadn't been today. This wind was going to play havoc with the precision flying they faced.

"We'll have to compensate for this wind, Nocturne," Jackson said quickly as the starting flag rose.

Nocturne's muscles bunched, and the sound her tail made against the asphalt was all the warning he needed. Jackson tensed. The flag dropped.

Despite all the practice take-offs and landings, the force of Nocturne's leap was like nothing Jackson had experienced before. He clung to the saddle, fighting a losing battle against the g-forces threatening to topple him from Nocturne's back. Utter horror consumed his thoughts.

This can't be happening.

CHAPTER FIFTY-NINE

JACKSON TEETERED ON THE EDGE OF DISASTER. The safety straps weren't going to be enough! He was going to fall, and his family would lose everything.

Nocturne dipped sharply, throwing Jackson forward, avoiding disaster. Scrambling to regain his seat, he groaned in shame. If it hadn't been for Nocturne, he would have failed them before they'd even started.

But there was no time to wallow in shame. The Arc de Triumph was coming up fast. One hundred sixty-four feet tall and one hundred forty-eight feet wide it stood in the middle of a huge traffic circle where eleven roads converged. The most notable being the Avenue de Champs-Èlysèes.

Vast crowds lined the broad avenue, cheering, waving flags, and jumping the barricades, their excitement on full display.

Jackson tightened his hands on the leather hand grips. They had to fly low enough not to break the infrared sensors at the top of each thirty-foot set of air-filled pylons while, more importantly, avoiding a direct hit to the famous monument.

The first pylon grew large, and Jackson had no time to

think as Nocturne barreled toward the obstacle. He tapped out the signal for her to slow. She didn't respond, and if anything, increased her speed.

The barrier was a blur as she made a quarter roll to the left. Her right wing came close to breaking the beam as she swooped left and then right to follow the multi-lane roundabout to the next barrier on the far side. With Nocturne's wing tip only inches from the ground, Jackson closed his eyes.

We're going too fast. We're going to crash!

LORELEI DANCED IN PLACE AS Nocturne cleared the second barrier and continued along the Champs-Èlysèes toward the next challenge. Jackson stayed stuck to the saddle like a tick on a dog. She glanced at Brandon, who continued to whoop and holler at one of the big screens set strategically along the course. He turned and lifted Lorelei off the ground, swung her around. His jubilation was simply too big to contain.

"Did you see that? Nocturne scraped the paint, coming and going. Rolled and twisted like a rainbow trout jumping for a Mayfly. Boyo never budged. What a ride." Brandon set Lorelei back on her feet and slapped a big kiss on her forehead.

"That it was." Lorelei's smile broadened. *I never had a doubt.*

WITH EACH TREMENDOUS FLAP OF her wings, the gleaming black rocket gathered speed while Jackson barely managed to keep his breakfast down. Nocturne was still ignoring his instructions, and Jackson had to accept that it was intentional. It hurt that he was being reduced to nothing more than an observer. His mum had told him to trust Nocturne, that she knew how to win. "Stay centered and do nothing to impede her effort."

Skimming along the treetops of the famous avenue, there was no time to linger on his near failure, and they flew too fast for him to marvel at his famous surroundings. The next obstacle lay at the end of the Champs-Èlysèes.

Nocturne's muscles were bunching in anticipation of the sharp right-hand turn that would mark the beginning of the obstacle that was the Place de la Concorde Plaza. Jackson adjusted his seat. He would not be caught unprepared again.

The oblong shape of the plaza was not the most difficult of the obstacles they would face before the day was done. Yet, intense concentration would still be needed on the part of the rider and dragon to stay low and tight while attempting a sharp right, then rolling left to follow the Plaza's first curve, and straightening out while maintaining speed at the optimum elevation before the next left curve, and finally a sharp right back onto the Champs-Èlysèes. Jackson barely had time to blink as Nocturne negotiated each pylon until, once again, they accelerated back the way they'd come.

After their first circuitous pass, the trip through the center of the Arc de Triomphe seemed like a cakewalk. Still, the sharp, high-speed turn that took them toward the Trocadero and the Eiffel Tower beyond wasn't exactly easy. However, the straight shot between obstacles gave Jackson a few minutes of respite before the most challenging and dangerous test on the course. But, it also gave him plenty of time to build up a boatload of anxiety.

It wasn't the string of thirty-foot pylons they passed through as they flew over the Trocadero gardens and its long row of fountains that Jackson dreaded. It was what lay at the end.

Gaining speed, Nocturne drove through the pylons,

crossed over the Seine River, and time was up. Jackson gasped as she powered through the last pylon and, without checking herself, rocketed straight up the side of the iconic monument. Her massive wings beat furiously as she fought against the gravity that fought just as hard to hold her down.

Vertical in the stirrups, Jackson clung to his dragon's surging body as she powered up the nearly vertical incline. The martingale, wrapped around her neck, cut into his fingers—spots formed in his vision. His chest felt like it was trapped in a vice, the jaws closing ever tighter.

Jackson's grip slipped as Nocturne topped the structure where a flag flapped in the wind—a banner they'd need to snag before descending the steel structure and the finish beyond.

Nocturne leveled out and circled the structure, preparing to grab the flag when a wind gust caught her massive wings and knocked them off course.

With a powerful downstroke, she banked sharply, snagged the flag in her foreclaw, and before Jackson could drag a breath into his heaving chest, she tucked her wings and plunged down the tower's opposite side.

Steel girders flashed by as they skimmed the surface. His feet in the dashboard, the back of the saddle digging into Jackson's spine, tears streamed from his eyes as they plummeted from the sky.

We're going to die!

CHAPTER SIXTY

FROM THE FREEFALL TO WAKING UP in his father's arms, Jackson couldn't recall what happened. What he *did* remember was abject terror.

"You alright? Can you stand?"

"What happened?" He struggled to get to his feet.

"You passed out." Aiden grimaced.

"We lost then." Jackson's shoulders slumped. "I don't think I'm cut out to be a jockey."

"Nope, you might have been hanging off the side of the saddle, but you were still in the strapping, which means you got a time. And that time was fast enough that you won the heat."

"No, it was Nocturne who won, and she did it without any help from me." He choked over the words. "I came so close to falling off before the race started that it's not even funny."

Lorelei grabbed Jackson by his shoulders and looked him in the eye. "Stop it, stop it right now." She pointed to where Nocturne relaxed in the straw. "I've never seen Nocturne fly like she did today. Speed has been her magic weapon, gymkhana her weakness." She held him at arm's length. Her features held a look of wonder. "But not today. Today, she was electrifying. Do you have any idea how few, if any, of those jockeys could have stayed aboard a dragon that moved like she did? They would have passed out from the g-forces long before you did."

A slight spark of warmth pushed at the ice encasing his heart—the day hadn't gone how he'd expected. Not even close. Strapped to Nocturne's back in an actual race was far more demanding than he had envisioned. *Would I have agreed to do this if I'd known?*

That was not a question that he could answer. But as he looked around at his family's grinning faces, he wasn't sure he'd ever climb on Nocturne's back again. His terror ran that deep, and he didn't know how to tell them.

A rustle in the straw drew his attention. Nocturne raised her head. Her golden eyes compelled him. He understood what she wanted. As he drew close, her massive muzzle nudged him to settle between her front legs, and as he did, she curled her neck protectively.

"Looks like the post-race talk is done." Brandon laughed.

"Now, what do you say we celebrate that three-minute fifty-two-second lead?" Cullum clapped a hand on Aiden's shoulder.

CHAPTER SIXTY-ONE

THE LACK OF LIGHT DID little to calm Sarah's terror as the storm raged around her. While a dark this deep would be helpful for someone who didn't want to be seen, such was not the case for Sarah. Her white hair and pale skin were as good as a lighthouse beacon on the darkest night.

Holding her breath, she tried to hear beyond the wild thumping of her pulse. If Toby caught her now, alone and without anyone to interfere on her behalf, she felt sure he would kill her. And she'd never been more certain of anything in her life. His hate and prejudice ran like a dark cancer through his soul.

With a last glance around, she scuttled from the perceived protection the hedge row offered and crossed the rain-slicked road to crouch at the base of the stack-stoned wall that surrounded the McLoughlin's farm.

A frantic scramble later, Sarah landed on the far side of the wall. Pulling the hood of her coat closer, she tucked away a few errant strands of hair that had escaped her ponytail before she sprinted into the open. She didn't slow until the black hulk of the dragon barns appeared ahead. A sliver of light flickered through the downpour as she drew closer, a guiding light for her frightened eyes. She'd made it. The stable doors were within reach. Now, if she could only get past the night watchmen.

Her chest heaving with each labored breath, Sarah stopped next to the pond where she, along with Jackson, Tivet, and Nocturne, had spent so many happy hours playing in the sun. Bending down, she scraped her fingers through the mud at the pond's edge, carefully she smeared it on her face, then rubbed the residue over her hands before she crept toward the barn's entry.

Peering through the juncture where the barn doors met, she lifted the latch and slipped into the warm interior. No one was around, but she didn't know how long that would last. According to the talk around the campfire, the McLoughlins had several watchmen, and between them, they patrolled around the clock.

And that wasn't all she'd learned hiding in the shadows. She'd also discovered what was planned for the next day's race. Hiding in the camp was no longer an option. The McLoughlins needed to be warned.

"Tivet," Sarah whispered as she stood outside his enclosure. Tivet reflected the light as brightly as Sarah's hair and skin. She marveled at the sight. He had grown far bigger than the last time she'd seen him. But that wasn't why she stared. His coat, scales, feathers, whatever they were, had grown more iridescent with a sheen that seemed to swirl within the shadows. He was genuinely breathtaking.

"When did you change so much?" Sarah slipped inside the stall. It had been weeks since she'd been to the farm, and there was no denying that Tivet was a sight to behold.

The dragonet rolled to his feet, his deep blue eyes dark in the dimness.

Sarah waited. She'd never been around Tivet without

Jackson. The straw rustled as he moved closer. Gently, he nuzzled her. His warm breath felt good against her frozen skin, and she, in turn, stroked the tiny scales that covered his face. She marveled at how sleek and soft they were against her fingers.

"Tivet, I need your help." He leaned in, and a sob clogged her throat. She had to swallow several times before she could continue. "You're the only one I can trust. They're laying a trap for Jackson and Nocturne in the final pass of the Labyrinth of Ruin. I don't know what they've planned or where it'll take place in the pass. I only heard them say that Lash would see to it that Nocturne wouldn't finish the race, and they'd used bookies to bet everything they had on Askook. You've got to warn them."

Tivet nudged the quietly weeping girl and looked past her to the door.

"Can you get there in time?" Sarah cupped his cheeks in her hands. Staring into his eyes, she waited for some form of confirmation. She had to know he would try.

The barn door opened and slammed against the outer wall. The gale's force was increasing. Sarah looked around frantically for a place to hide in the wide-open stall.

Tivet sank to the floor and raised his wing. Sarah dropped to her knees, and Tivet's wing folded over her body.

Moments later, the bright light of a high-powered torch illuminated the stall, flashing light into each corner and over Tivet twice.

"Sorry to disturb you, little one, just doing my job. I'm afraid the storm is only going to get worse. But don't you be frightened now. We've seen worse." Switching off the torch, the watchman left, the bang of the barn door a harsh exclamation in the quiet barn.

Sarah crept out from under Tivet's wing and rolled back the stall door. Tivet followed close on her heels. Down the shed row they went until they stood before the entrance. Reaching her fingers through the opening, she lifted the latch, and another gust of wind caught the door and tore it from her grasp. The crash against the outer wall seemed twice as loud as the others. Off to her right, through the driving rain, Sarah saw the tell-tale flash of his torch as the watchman turned back.

"Hey!" He shouted.

"Hurry." Sarah jumped aside as Tivet burst past her and, within a few steps, was arrowing up into the maelstrom. His body quickly taking on the sky's color and disappearing from Sarah's sight.

Sarah didn't wait and ran as fast as she could into a night that was so dark and filled with terror for her. But as she put distance between herself and the watchman's bobbing torch, a tiny spark of hope directed her steps.

CHAPTER SIXTY-TWO

THE FINAL DAY OF RACING HAD started like the previous two, with a dazzling spectacle of color and noise. For Jackson, the novelty had worn off on the first day, and it served only as an irritating distraction as he and Nocturne trembled in anticipation beneath the starting banner hours before.

Second in the standings, it seemed like an eternity had passed before the flag finally dropped and they were allowed to launch. In reality, it had been precisely four minutes and twenty-two seconds, the lead Duffy Nolan's dragon, Askook, enjoyed following the previous two days of racing.

But at this point in the race, Jackson wished, right to the tip of his frozen nose, that he and Nocturne still stood at that starting line. With a biting crosswind, each raindrop was as painful as a shard of ice at the speed they traveled. The oil-skin barrier of Jackson's rain gear offered little protection in these conditions.

Swiping at his goggles, he peered through the blurry mess. According to his compass, they were still headed in the right direction.

Nocturne was flying comfortably; the soft boom of each

downstroke was evenly paced. They had yet to spot Askook, and Jackson's chest tightened with the passage of each mile. Four minutes and twenty-two seconds in a race like this seemed like a lifetime. Askook had proved far faster than anyone had anticipated for a dragon his age and size. It would take everything Nocturne had to catch him, which meant taking risks while making friends with danger.

Slumped in the harness, Jackson realized he wasn't sure he had it in him to ask this of the courageous dragon beneath him. Or himself, for that matter.

The wind howled like a living entity, and in the distance, flashes of lightning lit the sky. Jackson couldn't dismiss that flying blind into the side of a mountain wasn't out of the realm of possibility if they were to throw caution to the wind.

Nocturne curved her head around. The slow blink of one golden eye and a flash of teeth were as good as the spoken word to lift his flagging spirits.

Perhaps Nocturne sensed his anxiety. His mum said dragons didn't need words to understand a rider's intent.

In that case . . . feel my intent. Jackson firmly placed an image in his mind of Askook struggling as Nocturne blew past him at the wire.

Nocturne roared, and her burst of flame lit the swollen sky as well as any bolt of lightning could.

CHAPTER SIXTY-THREE

RISING AND FALLING LIKE A runaway rollercoaster left Jackson slack in the saddle. He'd rechecked the safety harness at their last stop before heading out over open water. It took a single one-hundred-foot freefall to realize the harness would never be tight enough to ease his fear. *At least there aren't any mountains in our path.*

Flitting and swooping like a barn swallow in the gale-force winds proved more than Jackson's stomach could take, and the only good thing about the driving rain was that it washed away the vomit.

With the roiling sea and swirling sky wearing the same shade of gunmetal gray, telling up from down had proven difficult and only added to his nausea.

Groping for one of two thermos bottles strapped to the saddle, Jackson wrested one free with fingers made numb and sausage-like from the cold. Yet, within minutes, the warm protein shake threatened to go the way of everything else. Swallowing hard, he tried to think of something else—anything else.

Rechecking the instruments, he quickly calculated their

location. They weren't far from the second mandatory checkpoint near Dover, where he and Nocturne would undergo another wellness check before continuing on to Scotland, where the dreaded Labyrinth of Ruin awaited.

"We're getting close. Keep your eyes peeled for the landing pad," Jackson yelled. Missing one of the mandatory thirty-minute rest stops would result in a disqualification. Jackson rested his hand on Nocturne's massive shoulder joint. The vibration beneath his palm remained fluid and effortless despite the wind's steady buffeting. Satisfied, he checked the other joint and felt slightly better about their chances.

Nocturne banked sharply. Jackson scrambled to recenter himself and got his first glimpse of the giant flag that marked the checkpoint. Hammered by wind gusts, she repeatedly re-angled her body to maintain the concentric spiral that, with each pass, would bring them closer to the ground. *Hopefully, I won't be covered in vomit when we land.*

The landing proved far trickier than any Jackson had experienced. Swaying from side to side, Nocturne struggled to level her wings, and there was nothing he could do to help other than remain centered—no easy feat. A wingtip slamming against the blacktop could result in a severe injury. And what a hard landing would do to her previously injured hindleg was not a thought Jackson wanted to linger over.

Nocturne's tail whipped as she hovered against the combined forces of gravity and wind. Jackson clung to the rigging, terrified the slightest movement could throw her into an out-of-control spin.

Once they'd settled within the circle, Nocturne's wings folded at her sides, Jackson slumped, exhausted, his fear further weakening his body.

"Do you need some help there?" Aiden appeared as Jackson struggled to unbuckle the harness. With what little feeling remained in his extremities, it took longer than he would have liked.

"Nah, I got this." As his words slurred, Jackson recognized it wasn't just his fingers that had grown numb.

"Nocturne looks great. How are you doing?" Aiden studied his brother as he slid to the ground on unsteady legs. "Tough going out there?"

Jackson sensed his brother's need for reassurance but couldn't find it within himself to answer.

Letting it go, Aiden extended a plastic-wrapped sandwich. At the same time, he eyed the suspicious clumps that peppered Jackson's riding gear.

"Hang onto that." Jackson refused the sandwich. "I need to use the loo while the officials check Nocturne over."

By the time Jackson returned, Aiden had already replaced the saddle cloth and reset the saddle. Grabbing the rub rag from Aiden's back pocket, Jackson cleaned the dragon's face, paying particular attention to the area around her eyes and nostrils.

"Eat the sandwich." Aiden pulled it from the pocket of Jackson's rain slicker. "You need the energy and I put two more in your pack. Be sure you eat them." He pointed at a couple of kids handing out colorful thermoses. "There's hot chocolate over there. Make good use of these minutes to refuel. I'll see to Nocturne."

Jackson took a big bite and maneuvered closer to his brother. Placing a hand on Nocturne's nostril, Jackson spoke to her. "You okay, big girl?"

"She's doing fine. The vets were impressed. Of course, they've only had Askook to compare her with." He shrugged. "They didn't say, but gauging by how happy they were with our girl, I wonder if that big-bodied bugger might be having a wee bit of trouble staying in the air. He's not as sleek as our beauty here." Aiden smiled fondly as he placed a kiss between Nocturne's eyes; her nostrils flared in response. "You'll be glad to hear you two have cut his lead in half."

"Young man, we need you in the medical tent." An official approached and pointed to a white tent painted with a large red cross. Jackson wasn't sure he wanted to go in there. Leaning precariously to one side, it looked fit to blow away with the next big wind gust.

"It's not just Nocturne who gets a medical check." Aiden pointed at a bucket filled with a thick mixture steaming in the cold air. "I'll see that she finishes her hot mash. Now off with you."

"Thanks, man." Jackson spread his arms across Nocturne's head and whispered in her ear. "And thank you." She leaned into his touch, nearly knocking him off his feet.

Aiden's laughter followed Jackson as he walked away.

CHAPTER SIXTY-FOUR

THOUGH FLYING OVER THE LAND was easier than the open water, the bad weather wasn't letting up as the miles disappeared beneath the steady rhythm of Nocturne's wings.

Jackson's eyes grew heavier, and keeping them open grew more challenging. His tired thoughts lingered on what had plagued him from their first day of racing and his disastrous performance at the start—how his complete incompetence had nearly resulted in their ultimate failure before they'd even begun.

He didn't know how long he'd been asleep when a brilliant flash of light seared his eyelids, and the earsplitting explosion that followed almost stopped his heart. Reeling in the saddle, disoriented and ill-prepared for Nocturne's instant plunge, the safety straps on the harness were the only thing that kept Jackson in the saddle.

Leveling out, only to stutter in the grip of a powerful updraft, the uneven thump of Nocturne's wings punctuated the thunder bumpers' concussive sound as she desperately tried to gain altitude against a force far greater than herself.

Powering through the storm's black underbelly, glimpses

of billowy white beckoned. Shafts of light pierced the heavy clouds with streaks of liquid gold.

Jackson marveled at what lay before him as they finally broke through and into the light.

A brilliant landscape stretched as far as infinity and beyond. A limitless blue sky held aloft by an ocean of cottony white that appeared so soft and inviting, its allure was undeniable.

But they couldn't stay aloft for long; the lack of oxygen at the height they flew quickly became apparent as Jackson's thoughts grew sluggish, Nocturne's wing beats slowed, and they began to sink back into the brilliant white mattress that had seemed so welcoming, but proved far less substantial than its visual promised. Slowly, the cold depths, where the sun no longer shone, reclaimed them. And back into the vortex they flew.

CHAPTER SIXTY-FIVE

CULLUM JERKED HIS BINOCULARS into place, focusing on what was little more than a shadow in the thick mist that covered the landscape at the point from which he watched.

"Askook," he whispered, disappointed that it wasn't the much smaller outline of Nocturne he saw in the mist. The report from the Scottish border checkpoint had Askook's lead on Nocturne halved again from the previous mandatory stop.

At this point, Jackson and Nocturne were running out of real estate if they were to catch the leader.

Cullum listened carefully to the wingbeats he couldn't see. Though muted, experience told him the cadence was off, if only slightly, and that didn't bode well for the creature that flew overhead. Was the massive dragon tiring, or was his rider trying to save his faltering mount for a desperate final push to the finish where Nocturne was sure to make her presence felt?

Lorelei waited halfway down the Labyrinth of Ruin, on the other side of the mountain from Cullum. She'd chosen the exact point where Nocturne had been so severely injured by Askook's sire in her last race. These two positions were where they reasoned any shenanigans that had been planned would take place. But to this point, neither he nor Lorelei had seen anyone or anything suspicious.

Askook's shadow had just topped the ridge when the sound of rapid-fire wing beats reached Cullum's ears. Repositioning his binoculars, he whooped in glee at a much smaller shadow moving rapidly through the mist to top the ridge. He grabbed the radio.

"They're coming," He shouted.

"Ten-four," Lorelei responded. "I can't see anything yet. Wait, the sun is breaking through. What? What is he doing?" The alarm in his wife's voice was as clear as if she'd been standing next to him.

"What's happening? Talk to me."

"No," Lorelei cried before only static remained.

Terrified, Cullum clawed his way up the steep slope toward the ridge. The last of the mist burned away, and he could see Nocturne's scales glistening like onyx in the sunlight as the dragon swooped out of sight down the other side. Cullum caught the barest glimpse of the tiny figure who clung to her back.

CHAPTER SIXTY-SIX

FLYING LOW OVER THE SCOTTISH LOWLANDS as they'd approached the mountain range, the harsh wind and pounding rain had been replaced by a patchy, fog-like mist. Drops of frigid moisture clung to Jackson's face.

Twice, through the roiling mist, Jackson had caught a brief glimpse of Askook. With each of these sightings, Nocturne had increased her speed unasked.

Spreading his hands over the courageous dragon's scales, he searched for an indication that her strength flagged. She had to be exhausted. But the powerful thrum beneath Jackson's palms eased his concerns, and a renewed hope warmed his chest.

Jackson squinted against the glare as Nocturne powered out of the oppressive mist to top Aonach Dubh's weathered quartzite summit. Sunshine sparked glints of silver over a series of tumbling waterfalls that carved a path down the mountain's sides.

His stomach dropped as Nocturne rocketed down the rugged terrain, plunging ever faster with each beat of her wings—his vision filled with a blur of color.

The Three Sisters of Glencoe—ragged, sharp-edged ridges and steep V-shaped gullies pitted with obstacles. Little would be left if Nocturne miscalculated and crashed into one of the many jagged outcroppings.

Jackson's anxiety ratcheted higher at a sudden stutter in Nocturne's rhythm. But the gigantic red dragon flying straight at them made him gasp in terror.

His mind faltered. The boulder-strewn ground was far too close—the gully walls too near.

"Climb!" Jackson screamed.

Nocturne arched her neck, and her body shuddered as she attempted to fight the gravity that had been their friend only moments before.

The fiery red dragon powered toward them, his claws extended, his maw gaping, razor-sharp teeth exposed. No matter what Nocturne did, it was too late. A collision was unavoidable.

~*He's here.*

"What?" Jackson gasped, stunned at the sound of an unfamiliar voice inside his head.

~*Tivet's here.* Nocturne—for clearly it could be no other—shrieked.

~*Roll.* Tivet's voice rang out. ~*Meet his claws with your own. It's the only way.*

~*Tivet?* Jackson couldn't believe what he was hearing.

~*I'm here, Jack. Ready yourself. Askook is upon you.*

~*What are you doing?*

~*Ashook is not the only danger.*

~*But . . .*

~*Don't look back, Jack. You have to win.*

~*I . . .* Anguish filled Jackson's thoughts.

~*Promise me.*

~*I . . .* There was something so final about Tivet's words.
~I can't.

~I can. Nocturne grunted as she tucked her wings and rolled. Jackson groaned as the safety rigging dug into his thighs and the leather straps he'd hastily twisted around his arms stripped away his flesh.

~At least we'll die together.

~We will not *die today, Jackson McLoughlin.* Nocturne roared within his mind.

⁂

WITH HIS EYES TRAINED ON THE eminent collision, Tivet nearly missed an ominous glint of gunmetal against the mountainside.

He dove to intercept what he was certain would be a projectile intended for Jackson and Nocturne. A loud bang and puff of smoke was the only warning before a painful punch to his soft underbelly caused Tivet to falter.

Ignoring the pain, he accelerated toward the rocky mountainside. He couldn't allow the saboteur to get off another shot. But his wings refused to behave the way they should. And as his legs began to sag and his tail drooped, Tivet faltered.

Though his vision wavered, he recognized the shooter partially concealed behind a bright yellow patch of gorse. Bent over, Lash fumbled with a feathered dart, trying to jam it into the rifle's loading mechanism.

I can still save Nocturne and Jackson.

Focusing on the spot, his flaccid wings no longer responding, Tivet trusted gravity to take care of the rest. His last clear thought was his love for Jackson and Nocturne, the only family he'd ever known.

The wide bore of the rifle and the man behind it was the last thing Tivet saw.

CHAPTER SIXTY-SEVEN

AS HELPLESS AS A STRAW-FILLED dummy, Jackson flailed about in the harness as Nocturne rolled to face Askook's attack.

Roars assaulted Jackson's ears, and the sulfurous smell of dragon fire made it hard to breathe.

Nocturne unfurled her wings, claws extended, and as the two dragons collided, a lance of fiery pain accompanied a loud pop in Jackson's left shoulder.

Askook's wing raked Nocturne's side, narrowly missing Jackson. Retaliating, Nocturne clamped her jaw into the leathery mass of the other dragon's wing. With a vicious turn of her head, a ragged line appeared in the membrane.

Askook roared, redoubling his efforts to tear the smaller dragon to pieces.

"Nocturne," Jackson howled as he felt his dragon falter.

~*He's gone.* Nocturne moaned. Her wings slackened as she hung suspended from Askook's claws.

Jackson's vision wavered. Abject grief flooded his senses. His connection to Tivet was severed.

Suddenly, Askook's jockey, coated in blood, hurtled past. His screams and the look of horror on his face shook Jackson to his soul. This was no game they played.

~Nocturne. Tivet needs us.

Her entire body convulsed, and she responded to Jackson's plea, viciously tearing into her attacker. This time, she managed to rend away a flap of wing sail, and he released her.

Roaring in outrage, Askook shot a spout of lava-red fire, filling the air between the combatants with flame. Nocturne contorted her body, taking the brunt of the fire with her left wing before somersaulting away faster than the red dragon could react.

Nocturne dropped from the sky with her black wings folded against her sides. There was no time to scream as the jagged boulder-strewn ground awaited. Jackson closed his eyes. It was the sharp sound of Nocturne's wings billowing with air that had him reopening them.

Nocturne leveled out to skim along the bottom of the gully. He got a glimpse of the mangled body of the man who had threatened him in the jock's room, the bright racing colors he wore, a garish statement against the lichen-covered rocks.

~Askook tore him from the saddle. Nocturne explained.

Although the man may have threatened Jackson and Nocturne before the race, that did not mean he deserved to die.

A thunderous roar snapped Jackson's attention back to their predicament. He and Nocturne were both injured. Askook's injury, if anything, only seemed to have made him more dangerous—he hadn't given up the chase.

~Nocturne, he's going to kill us.

~Steady, young Jackson. Don't despair. He'll have to catch us first. We'll stay low to the ground. He'll hesitate to sacrifice himself in such close quarters and he will wait until we're forced into the open.

How could Jackson not despair? His arm had gone numb and lay useless in the harness straps. And compounding the situation, with each twist, turn, and dip over the rough terrain, he felt himself growing weaker. Nocturne would be better off without him.

~*Jackson. I need you to help me.*

~*What can I do? I have nothing left to give. I never really did.*

~*It was your faith in me that brought me back from my despair. Despite the pain, your faith got me off the ground, and your continued belief in me will get us through this race. Please, Jackson, I can't do this without you.*

As they passed over a waterfall and the ground dropped away, Askook's massive shadow blotted out the sun.

"Dive!" Jackson screamed. Nocturne spiraled, her wings tucked so close to her sides Jackson could have grasped the wing claws.

Askook's bulk cleaved the air as he slammed past, his claws within inches of connecting.

Nocturne groaned, her head dipping as she was slow to regain control.

~*Are you hurt?*

~*Yes. His tail spike reopened the scar on my leg.*

~*You need to land.*

~*The finish is only a few miles away, and my leg will not slow my wings.*

~*Nocturne, you're all that matters.*

~*Tivet sacrificed himself so we could finish.*

~*You're right, we have to finish.* "For Tivet," Jackson screamed.

~*Where's Askook?* Nocturne swiveled her head from side to side, scanning the landscape. ~*I don't see him.*

~*I don't see him either. Is he at the bottom of the cliff, or could he have gone into the water?*

~*Either way, let's hope he did.* Nocturne headed for the mouth of the valley and the finish line that lay beyond.

CHAPTER SIXTY-EIGHT

Four weeks later—

JACKSON OPENED HIS EYES TO bluebird skies and the raucous sounds of laughter and camaraderie filling the warm summer air. Lifting his head, he shaded his eyes. Aiden and Robby, each with a long-handled utensil, were engaged in good-natured sniping on the best way to cook the steak and sausages that sizzled over the flames.

A large splash drew his attention to the pond where Tivet, sporting a very long and strange-looking cervical collar, awkwardly tried to bypass an anxious Nocturne who seemed intent on keeping the still-recovering dragonet at the shallow end of the pond.

Jackson's lips tightened as his eyes settled on the still angry-looking scar on Nocturne's leg. The sight triggered vivid memories of the race's final moments, even now four weeks later. The race they'd barely survived.

As the first team to finish, the crowd greeted Nocturne and Jackson with uproarious cheers while a band played and a cloud of colorful balloons were released into the sky. However, those shouts of joy quickly turned to screams of horror as Nocturne's injured leg failed to hold. While Jackson hung limply to one side, the bloodied duo skidded across the ground, the crowd scurrying to get out of their path. His last memory was his brother running toward him, screaming for the race medics.

The next time Jackson woke, he was in a hospital bed, his parents at his side.

"Tivet and Nocturne are both alive," his mother's first words—so like her to anticipate and soothe his biggest fear. Tears running down her face, she hadn't tried to hug him, for there wasn't any place on his body that didn't hurt.

"You, however, have a good deal of healing to do." Lorelei had gently run her fingers over the bandage covering the left side of his head. "And no small amount of hair to grow back."

And it was his mother's voice that interrupted his reverie, calling out. "Look who just arrived, mo chrói."

As they approached the lawn chair where he rested, Jackson's smile grew at the sight of Sarah and her Ya Ya, Fawnie Coffey. It couldn't have been easy for Fawnie, with her son Lash dead and her grandson Toby detained in a youth detention school for the foreseeable future. But here they were.

They'd visited once while he was still in hospital, but it had been hard to concentrate with his dislocated shoulder and a pair of fractured ribs that still twinged and ached twenty-four hours a day. And then there were the dragon fire burns that would have been far worse if Nocturne hadn't protected him by taking the brunt of the fire. His eyes flicked to the black dragon, who now watched him from the pond's edge.

~*We will all heal and fly again,* Ceann Cróga.

~*Brave One?* Jackson snorted and waved her back to guarding Tivet.

A lot had happened while Jackson was being treated for

his injuries. Lash Coffey, Sarah's father, who died from injuries he'd sustained when a tranquilized Tivet crashed into the mountainside, had been buried, as well as Sammy Doyle, Askook's jockey.

Due to these deaths, official inquiries into what happened before, during, and after the Labyrinth of Ruin led to a full-scale government investigation that revealed widespread illegalities involving nearly every aspect of racing on the European scene.

The involvement of organized crime, once only whispered about, was now openly being investigated. Racing officials, owners, and trainers like Duffy Nolan and Connor Doyle, jockeys like the deceased Sammy Doyle, and even veterinarians were being looked at after a necropsy of Askook's body revealed the presence of banned substances. Duffy's holdings had been seized as the tax authorities brought tax fraud allegations.

A diesel engine's roar disturbed the tranquility along with Jackson's musings. He grunted as he leaned forward to take a closer look at the dragon transport as it pulled up to the quarantine barn.

"Come on, son. It's time to get up." Cullum handed Jackson a cane. "We have a surprise for you."

"A surprise?" *What kind of surprise would be arriving in a dragon transport?*

~They better not think they can replace us. Tivet piped up.

Jackson suppressed a bark of laughter at the dragonet's snark. He and Nocturne were standing at the edge of the pond. Their joint suspicion and indignation were evident in their very puffed-up bodies.

~The world will end before that happens . . . maybe not even then. Jackson smiled, clasping Sarah's hand, he hobbled after his father.

The transport rocked on its axles as a further four trucks

began lining up in the lane. The massive diesel's passenger door opened, and Regan Malony climbed down from the cab and strode over to shake Cullum's hand.

"So . . ." Regan glanced down at Jackson. "This is my new jockey? I've heard his book will be full by the time he's healed. I want to get my name on the list before that happens."

"I'm creature deaf, you know that," Jackson sputtered.

"That's not what I heard." Regan looked over to the pond and pointed. "Right over there's proof to the contrary."

"They're special."

"As are you, young man." Regan looked away as the tailgate was lowered on the first transport, and a familiar dark brown dragon swaggered down the ramp.

"Mr. Malony, I can't communicate with your dragons nor anybody else's."

Luna stopped on her way to the barn. A coppery sheen glistened off her scales as she preened in the sun. Jackson caught his breath in wonder. *She's more beautiful than ever.*

~You dare speak to me? Luna whipped her head around, then twitched her tail and stalked off.

~Tivet, she heard me. Jackson was stunned.

~Of course she did. We taught you to speak dragon. But you're still ours and don't forget who's really important. A burst of joy filled Jackson's senses, and he turned in time to see the mud-stained white dragonet dash past Nocturne to jump back into the water.

Snorting her outrage, Nocturne stomped along the edge of the pond.

"Da." Jackson tugged on his hand. "I heard Luna."

"I figured you might." He shrugged. "It stood to reason that once you learned to speak with Nocturne, it wouldn't stop there."

"Okay. But how did Mr. Malony know I could talk with dragons?"

"Son, this is Ireland. If one person knows a secret, then everybody knows."

"That's the truth of it." Sarah released his hand and was headed for the pond.

"Hey, Sarah, wait up."

She stopped, her shy smile as bright as the world around her.

The farm is safe, Sarah is safe, and I have a family that loves me.

~Hey, we're family too. Tivet intruded into his thoughts.

~Exactly.

The End

Characters

JACKSON MCLOUGHLIN — Youngest son of Cullum and Lorelei McLoughlin

TIVET — Adopted by Jackson, and a dragonet like no other

CULLUM MCLOUGHLIN — Father to Jackson McLoughlin; Dragon Speaker, Breeder, and trainer of racing dragons

LORELEI MCLOUGHLIN — Mother of Jackson McLoughlin; Dragon Speaker, Breeder, trainer and retired Dragon jockey

ROBBY — Jackson's oldest brother; Dragon Speaker, Breeder and trainer of racing dragons

AIDAN — Jackson's second oldest brother; Dragon Speaker, Breeder and trainer of racing dragons

BRANDON — Jackson's third oldest brother, Dragon Speaker, Breeder and trainer of racing dragons

DOC MILLER — Veterinarian and close family friend

TOBY COFFEY — A Traveller and the same age as Jackson

SARAH COFFEY — A Traveller and a friend of Jackson

LASH COFFEY — A Traveller and father to Lash and Sarah

FAWNIE COFFEY — Lash's mother

REGAN MALONY — Cullum's best client

DUFFY NOLAN — Owner of Nolan Racing

RORY WALSH — The Garda of the local Garda Síochána

HARRIS FLYNN — Jockey

CONNOR DOYLE — Duffy Nolan's Irish trainer

SHAMUS SMYTH — A dragon trainer

SAMMY DOYLE — Jockey

ASKOOK — Dragon

NOCTURNE — Dragon

LUNA — Dragon

NIGHTWING — Dragon

SCYLLAR — Dragon

Glossary

Abattoir — Meat processing plant
Acting the maggot — slang for acting like an idiot
Aga — A brand of range cooker, more commonly called a stove in the United States
Bacon Baps — A simple bacon sandwich
Claiming Race — A race in which a dragon can be claimed for the amount specified in the conditions
Compeer — A companion or associate
Creature Deaf — The offspring of a Dragon Speaker who cannot communicate with the dragons
Cully — A friend
Daoir-darn — A mild expletive
Day Money — Training fees
Dosh — A working-class term for money
Dragon Hunters — Those who hunt dragons out of hatred and greed
Dragon Speakers — Are those humans born with the ability to communicate with dragons
Drakaina — A female dragon
Eejit — Informal Northern Irish term for an idiot
Gob — Slang for the mouth
Graded Stakes Race — A top-level race as in Thoroughbred racing, and they are often named races, like the Queen's Plate, Kentucky Derby, and many other prestigious races
Ifrinn — Irish explative
Irish Cobs — A small, solidly built horse and is often Piebald in coloring. (Piebald — typically containing black and white irregular patches of color)
Maiden Race — A race written solely for dragons who have never won a race
Máthair — Mother
Mí-ádh — Ill luck
Mo chrói — Irish for my hear
Natter — Talk casually, chatter

Pebbledash — A rough plaster surface made from a variety of materials, including sand and small stones, then applied to the exterior surface of a home

Pingin' — Irish penny

Pound — Another term for money in certain parts of the world

Punters — A gambler who places a bet

Quid — Irish term for paper money in reference to a pound note

Rotter — British slang for a person perceived to be worthless, despicable, or unpleasant

Scut — Slang for a worthless, contemptible person

Slag heap — A hill or mound made of industrial refuse

Slurry Pit — An area that a farmer reserves for the collection of animal waste

Sod — A playful word for person

Spinney — A small area of trees and shrubs, often found near running water

Stakes Race — A top-level race, often written with conditions

Stealth Dragons — Icelandic Sleek-Backed Swift, also known as a Death Spectre

Submarined — A trainer who is finagled out of their customers by a competitor

Teach Mór — A type of historic home

Tetchier — slang for bad tempered and irritable

Timothy Hay — An abundant perineal grass native to Europe

Travellers — An ethnic group who adhere to a nomadic way of life

Whinging — slang for whining or complaining

Wings Jerked Off — A euphemism for getting beat by a significant distance in a race or workout

Ya Ya — Grandmother

Reviews and Other Works

Reviews are the heart blood of every writer. If you liked Jackson and Tivet's story, please consider leaving a review. I read every one, and often more than once.

Other works by Shelley Lee Riley:

Casual Lies—A Triple Crown Adventure
The true story of Stanley, a head-strong, charismatic Thoroughbred who helped turn a horse-obsessed girl into a history-making woman.

Into Madness—Born From Stone Saga #1
Brought together by circumstance. Forged together by fate. Will it be enough to save the world?
Princess Ravinia Carolingian, trapped by her enemy, must first escape King Grigorii Mercoviche before she can reclaim her kingdom and save the Carolingian people from the evil that threatens them all.

About the Author

Shelley Lee Riley is the International award-winning author of *Casual Lies—A Triple Crown Adventure*. The memoir tells her personal story about Casual Lies, the horse she trained through all three American Triple Crown Races—the first woman to do so. Following five years in the United Kingdom, she returned to the San Francisco Bay Area and, in her spare time, worked as a freelance writer for various publications. Now retired in Oregon, she enjoys living in a forest, watching the deer clearcut the garden, the sounds of the Canadian geese roosting on the chimney, and the squirrels chewing the siding, the decking, and the sprinkler heads. While not engaged in repairs and replacement gardening, she enjoys writing fiction.

Follow Shelley at: www.shelleyleeriley.com

www.ingramcontent.com/pod-product-compliance
Lightning Source LLC
Chambersburg PA
CBHW020550180626
46810CB00007B/2450